"Freeze!"

The three men bolting toward Carl Lyons, guns flashing, had picked the wrong man at the wrong time if they hoped for an easy surrender. With a banshee cry, the Able Team warrior unleashed his pent-up emotions in a limb-flailing display of Shotokan karate. The gunman closest to him crumpled to the carpet with the wind knocked from his lungs. A second man took a blow to the side of the head that sent him reeling against the wall. But Lyons only had two arms and legs and could not disable the final attacker before the butt of an automatic pistol clipped him behind the right ear.

Already off balance, the Ironman staggered awkwardly to one side, bowling over a potted rubber plant as he fought to retain consciousness. It was a losing battle, and within seconds Lyons had succumbed to the creeping void.

Mack Bolan's

ABLE TEAM®

ABLE TEAM.
Red Menace

Dick Stivers

A GOLD EAGLE BOOK FROM
WORLDWIDE.

TORONTO · NEW YORK · LONDON · PARIS
AMSTERDAM · STOCKHOLM · HAMBURG
ATHENS · MILAN · TOKYO · SYDNEY

First edition August 1988

ISBN 0-373-61237-0

Special thanks and acknowledgment to
Ron Renauld for his contribution to this work.

PROLOGUE

...and although you're away
In my heart you'll stay,
And each day I'll be thinking
About you...

As the crowd howled excitedly, Roxanne Darling sang her most recent hit on the country charts and moved to the front of the stage, making eye contact with as many servicemen as possible. Even though the flood-lights half blinded her, she could see numerous faces in the first few rows. Young faces, most of them American, all of them showing obvious relief at this chance to spend a few hours away from their grim duty of keeping the peace in San Leon. Some of the servicemen had been here in Central America for almost a year, part of the United Nations force stationed in that small country in hopes of defusing the powderkeg political tensions in the region and preventing civil war. It was a thankless task, for these uniformed peacekeepers were scorned by the citizenry and despised by local political factions.

"Yeah!" one of the soldiers cried out to Roxanne. "Sing it, girl!"

"I'm tryin', darlin'," Roxanne teased good-naturedly between lyrics, earning yet another chorus of whoops from the sea of manpower filling the makeshift stands on the edge of the army base. Nearby, a renovated DC-8 rested on the tarmac of an airfield, towering over the Iroquois choppers and smaller reconnaissance planes used by the U.N. as part of its mission. Beyond the airstrip, a barrier of barbed wire and reinforced fence separated the compound from the capital, San Leon City, visible as a distant dome of light that rose into the cloudless night sky.

Roxanne Darling was the headliner on a ten-act bill assembled by the USO, and she had already lived up to the day-long anticipation. So far, she had performed nineteen songs from the numerous best-selling albums she'd released since attaining prominence after an impromptu performance at Nashville's Grand Ole Opry five years earlier. Fame had done little to change her sprightly, cheerful demeanor, and although she wore a costume of tailored silk and glittering sequins with color-coordinated boots and guitar, there was still an air of unpretentious innocence about her. Her voice was equally pure, giving a credibility to lyrics that might have seemed hopelessly saccharine when sung by others.

Not to say that there wasn't a fair share of lust in the hearts of men in the crowd, who longed for the soft touch of a woman. Most of the whistles and howls were meant as a compliment to the singer's lush strawberry-blond curls and her trim, athletic figure, which swayed so effortlessly in time to the music.

"We love you, Roxanne!" another man yelled above the applause when the song had ended.

"Marry me!" came a lovesick yelp from the back row.

Roxanne blushed at the adulation and smiled gratefully as she tuned her guitar and waited for the crowd to quiet down. "I want to thank you all for being such kind gentlemen," she said with a sly wink, extending the drawl in her Tennessee accent. "I just hope that when you all get a chance to come home, you'll come see one of my shows in the States. They don't have curfews there and I can play a little longer." She waited out an outburst of cheers and howls, then strummed the opening chords of her biggest hit and continued, "But for now, I'm gonna have to leave you with one of my favorites, and I'm sure that if your gals could talk to you now, they'd agree with me that

> True hearts stay close
> Even when they're far away.
> True hearts stay close
> Forever and a day..."

FIVE MILES AWAY, Roxanne's thirty-year-old brother strode cautiously down the side streets of San Leon City, pulse racing with each tentative step. Brian Darling had shed his satin USO tour jacket and the laminated name tag identifying him as a member of Roxanne Darling's road crew. His sister's show, after all, was not his reason for being in Central America. Much as he admired Roxanne's morale-boosting activities with the U.N. troops, Brian considered his own secret mission as being potentially far more influential to the region.

And it was certainly more dangerous.

Wearing the stiff-fabric peasant garb of a San Leon field-worker, his features hidden beneath the brim of a straw sombrero, Brian hunched slightly to downplay his six-foot height and tried to blend in with the native townspeople as best he could, knowing full well that he was far removed from the protection of the army camp. Since slipping away from the base, he'd encountered only one jeep load of U.N. soldiers. If trouble arose, there was no guarantee he'd be able to find assistance in time to avoid the consequences.

San Leon City was under limited martial law, and the nightly curfew would be in effect in less than an hour. Now, however, the streets teemed with activity, providing Brian with adequate cover. This being the feast day of St. Leon, the populace was in a rare celebratory mood, and much of that celebrating took place beneath the stars. Snatches from a dozen folk songs filtered down dusty alleys, accompanied by the strains of guitars and the rattle of mariachis. A procession down the main road featured huge papier-mâché figures of St. Leon and his attendant angels, and ceremonial piñatas dangled at the end of handheld poles, bound for the town square, where children would beat them open with sticks and then scramble for the sweets and small toys hidden inside. Hours before, the street had been carpeted with elaborate patterns of dyed sawdust, and now the trodden colors bled into one another as if the San Leonians were marching over a shattered rainbow.

The aroma of late supper offerings wafted in the light breeze that crossed the city. Brian detected the scent of frijoles, enchiladas and freshly-made tortillas, reminding him that he hadn't eaten since afternoon. He'd missed supper call at the base, using that time to start out on foot for the city. The long hike had taken a toll on his sandaled feet, and the thongs' leather straps chafed at blisters on his toes and ankles. He endured the pain but not his hunger pangs. Once he reached the edge of the town square, he bought a chile relleno at a corner stand run by a weary-faced woman and her daughter. Fortunately, he'd changed a few American dollars into pesos upon arriving in the country, so he could pay without causing a scene. The girl stared intently at Brian, however, and he quickly moved away when she tugged at her mother's blouse and whispered something in her ear.

Standing in the shadows, Brian ate slowly as he watched the activity in the square, which was surrounded by one- and two-story adobe buildings, most of them erected in the aftermath of civil war uprisings three years ago and a major earthquake a decade before that. The procession had arrived and there was much merriment around the piñatas as they were cracked open. Shrieking children scrambled in the dirt for fallen treasures, scattering stray, squawking chickens in their wake. Village elders watched with smiles on their weathered faces, recalling their own distant youth in the days when there was peace in San

Leon. Revelers across the way danced by torchlight beneath the slowly sweeping hands of the new mission clock, which counted the minutes until curfew.

This was how it should be for them every night, Brian mused. Free to enjoy life without the threat of war or the worry about running afoul of San Leon's dreaded secret police, El Chocomil del Sangre. Originally an enforcement arm of General Marcos Pabro during his brief and brutal reign over the country, El Chocomil had remained in existence after the overthrow of Pabro and the reinstatement of democracy in San Leon. With Pabro imprisoned, the secret police were testing the electoral waters with various puppet governments. Although U.N. influence was making headway in easing open hostilities in this part of Central America, Brian knew that El Chocomil still operated with few restraints, primarily because it acted clandestinely, without the official recognition or sanction of the local government. It was a shadow entity, but its dire effects were no illusion. Those who spoke out against El Chocomil had a way of mysteriously vanishing during the dead of night, or sometimes even during the harsh glare of day, never to be seen again. Backed by U.N. troops, fact-finding groups had searched the nation's prison system for a trace of the missing, invariably without luck. Rumors persisted that El Chocomil utilized secret prisons... and unmarked grave sites for those who died during torture or interrogation.

Brian Darling was in San Leon to help blow the lid off El Chocomil del Sangre.

As part of the investigatory arm of the United States-based Crusade for Conscience, Brian was devoted to the cause of exposing human rights violations around the globe. Assigned out of the agency's Nashville office to concentrate on the San Leon region, he'd spent almost fifteen months cultivating long-distance connections with key Central American figures sharing the same goals as the CFC. The work had paid off, for his network of contacts finally led him to a one-time member of El Chocomil who had fled from his duties as a guard at one of the secret police's main detention camps in the hills outside San Leon City. The man was prepared to turn over extensive documentation on El Chocomil activities, including photographs he'd managed to take prior to fleeing the camp. Tonight, Brian was to meet both Louis Herton, the former guard, and his San Leon contact, David Keliersa, a local folksinger known for his stirring anthems proclaiming the need for freedom throughout Central America.

At a quarter to ten, Brian quietly pushed through the throng in the square and went to Avenida Missione, a dark and nearly deserted part of town. A small contingent of *federales* marched out of the darkness toward him, bound for the square to enforce the curfew. Brian cast his eyes downward to avoid the soldiers' gazes and to calm the unsettled feeling in his stomach. The *federales* passed him without incident, but Brian's nervousness was slow to depart. Because the Crusade for Conscience was an organization predicated on the belief in nonviolence,

Brian was unarmed, and he felt increasingly vulnerable as he walked alone through the industrial section of town.

Counting buildings, Brian came to an arched gateway leading to a small darkened courtyard within a closed-down factory complex. Weeds had long ago overrun the landscaping, and vandals had broken the four stone benches that faced a small well, and most of the factory windows. Brian hesitated a moment outside the arch, battling his fear. When two figures emerged from the shadows near the well, Darling shivered.

One of the duo whispered to Brian in a foreign language, asking him what sort of weather he thought the clouds might bring. Brian sighed with relief and responded to the coded query with a few words of the local dialect he'd learned in preparation for this rendezvous.

"Lluvia de oro," he said. Rain of gold.

"Ah, Brian! Come, come...."

He passed beneath the arch and joined the others at the well. David Keliersa was tall and lean, a third-generation San Leonian with dark hair and the characteristic long, thin sideburns favored by men in the city. Louis Herton, by contrast, was squat and round-faced, with small eyes and a thick mustache. They both eyed Brian intently. Darling took off his sombrero and set it on the rim of the well. Pale-faced with a receding hairline and hawklike nose, Darling usually looked a decade older than he actually was. Tonight he seemed even more aged.

"At last we meet in the flesh," Keliersa said as he shook Brian's hand. "I have been looking forward to it."

"Me, too," Brian said. He nodded as he was introduced to Herton, then asked the guard, "You brought the information?"

"*Sí.*" Herton reached inside his loose overcoat, removing a packet the size of a tobacco pouch. He handed it to Brian. "Here," he said with a thick, broken accent. "And I have something else, too."

"The photos?" Brian asked.

"No..." Herton jerked out a Colt Cobra Model D3 and stepped back as he waved the revolver at the two younger men. "This!"

"What are you doing?!" Brian exclaimed, dumbfounded by the sight of the .38.

By way of answering, Herton snapped his fingers, signaling gunmen hiding inside the abandoned factory. A spotlight situated in one of the windows suddenly shot a wide glaring beam into the courtyard, exposing the three men by the well.

"It's a trap!" Keliersa shouted as he instinctively lunged for the man who had betrayed him. Herton managed to fire one shot before Keliersa was on him, and the San Leonian let out an involuntary cry of pain as a 200-grain slug slammed into his ribs. As the two men tumbled to the ground, Brian hurriedly ducked behind the well, avoiding the gunfire coming from the second story of the factory.

In the struggle, Keliersa knocked Herton's revolver aside and it clattered through the weeds to within

Brian's reach. He stared at the weapon, unsure of what to do.

"Knock out the light and run for it!" the wounded Keliersa gasped, still subduing the round-faced guard. It looked like only a matter of seconds before Herton would shake the man off him.

During his thirty years in Nashville, Brian Darling had never faced a life-and-death situation. It had been relatively easy to hold a nonviolence stance. But now that stance seemed to be crumbling instantaneously, as his present situation argued for a violent resolution. More bullets chewed through the weeds to his left. Brian knew, as sure as he was squatting there, that he and Keliersa were doomed unless he took action.

Grabbing the Cobra, Brian aimed its 101 mm barrel at the spotlight and squeezed the trigger, feeling the gun buck in his hand like something alive. The first shot flew wide. Tightening his grip, he fired again, this time managing to take out the spotlight. The last image he saw before darkness swept back over the courtyard was that of Louis Herton rising from the ground where David Keliersa lay, and lumbering toward the well.

"No!" Brian hissed, firing point-blank at the former guard. That close, he couldn't help but nail Herton, who cursed as he teetered headlong to the ground near one of the broken benches.

The unseen gunmen continued firing blindly from their sniper posts in the factory, and Brian instinctively knew that it was only a matter of time before they got him, one way or another. He knew he had no choice but to follow Keliersa's advice and flee.

Drawing in a quick breath, Brian fired another upward shot, then bolted from cover and charged for the archway. Gunfire peppered the ground around him but he managed to reach the opening unscathed. Without pausing, he took to the street, kicking off his sandals so they wouldn't slow him down.

"Stop!" shouted a uniformed man as he stepped out of a doorway and blocked Brian's way.

Reckless in his fear, Darling ignored the other man's weapon and brought up Herton's Cobra D3, emptying the last rounds. With a stunned grunt, the man spun halfway around and fell, wasting shots into the dirt as Brian hurried past.

A track star in high school and college, Darling was no stranger to sprints, and although he wasn't in prime physical shape, the Nashville man quickly lengthened the distance between himself and the gunmen who filed out of the factory and chased him down San Leon City's side streets. The din of small-caliber retorts caromed off the walls, and several times Brian heard bullets skim off the brick and adobe around him. He ran all the faster, determined that one of those slugs wasn't going to have his name on it.

Reaching the town square, Brian cast aside the emptied gun and used the gathered throng for cover, crouching low as he caught his breath and weaved through the unsuspecting celebrants, heading toward a U.N. Jeep idling on the side of the road out of the city. There was only one man inside the vehicle and, fortunately for Brian, he was an American.

"Help!" he wheezed, jumping into the back of the Jeep and hiding. "You have to get me back to the base!"

"What's the problem?" the driver asked casually.

"You and I are going to be dead meat if we stay here, that's the problem! Now get us out of here!"

The driver glanced across the town square, seeing the handful of men converging upon the crowd from Avenida Missione. Shifting the Jeep into first, he drove off, waiting until they were leaving the city behind before chancing a glance over his shoulder and asking Brian, "You better start thinking fast, fella, because you're gonna have yourself some explaining to do when we get back to the base, ace . . ."

SERGEANT JUAN GUANDARO was sitting on the terrace of El Aquila, the most expensive restaurant in San Leon. A thick-bellied bearded man, Guandaro had a taste for the finer things in life, and this evening that taste had been appeased by two rare sirloin steaks, a rasher of bacon grilled with diced red potatoes, three ears of sweet corn, a pork burrito and three small baskets of fresh-baked dinner rolls. To wash down this feast he had consumed a magnum of Dom Perignon and a quart of milk. Now he contemplated dessert as he leered across the table at his dinner companion, a sleek, light-skinned, Salvadoran woman of rare beauty, who was paid handsomely to flatter the sergeant in public and to please him in private. She performed both tasks with dazzling finesse.

"You barely touched your food, Maria," Guandaro boomed in his deep, husky voice as he wiped his fingers on the linen napkin draped across his tailor-made slacks. Though he was a military man through and through, Guandaro wandered San Leon City in civilian dress, downplaying his previous association with deposed dictator Pabro.

Maria longed to tell him that when one watched a pig at the trough it was difficult to have much of an appetite, but she knew better than to speak her mind. Instead, she responded with a sultry whisper, "I am only hungry for you, Juan."

"Then I will be your dessert." Guandaro chuckled, reaching inside his coat for a long cigar as thick as his index finger. He added, "And you will be mine...."

From the terrace, which overlooked the town square, Guandaro glanced toward Avenida Missione as he lit his cigar. The smile left his face and he waved out his match as he saw two of his men rushing from the street into the crowd. Dressed in plain slacks and lightweight overcoats, the men ran through the townsfolk, their heads high as though on the lookout. They carried Ingram Model 10 submachine guns and made little effort to conceal them. Already citizens were recoiling from the men in both fear and indignation.

"Idiots!" he cursed, as he pushed away from the table. "Put those guns away!"

Almost as if they had heard him, the two men secreted the weapons inside their coats and turned, steering wide of the *federales* and the U.N. officers positioned near a large statue of St. Leon in the middle of the square.

"What's wrong, Juan?" Maria asked.

Guandaro made no answer. He guided his bulk past the patrons next to him and headed for the stairway leading down to the plaza. On the way, he motioned to the maître d' and snapped, "See that the woman is given a ride home and put it on my tab."

As he was heading down the steps, making the wood slats groan under his 230 pounds, one of his men entered the stairwell and bounded up to meet him. Guandaro was about to berate the underling's reckless display of the submachine gun when the other man spoke.

"Sergeant Guandaro, come quick! We have a problem!"

"No brains between your ears, that is the problem!" Guandaro snapped. "It's a miracle that you weren't seen waving your Ingram by—"

"Your brother," the man in the coat interrupted. "He's been shot!"

"Tomas?" Guandaro was stunned, and the color drained from his face. "Where is he?" he demanded.

"Near the courtyard. There was a problem with the ambush. Jorge is already dead and—"

The sergeant lashed out with a swiftness amazing for a man his size, hitting the shorter man in the chest and nearly bowling him over the railing. The sergeant stormed past him and down to the plaza. With only minutes to go before curfew, the *federales* were dispersing the crowd, and Guandaro encountered little resistance as he strode forcefully across the square to Avenida Missione and proceeded to the abandoned factory where he had ordered his men to ambush the enemies that Louis Herton had promised to bring them. To Juan Guandaro, anyone opposed to El Chocomil del Sangre was an enemy. Indeed, since the untimely demise of General Pabro, Juan Guandaro ruled the secret police of San Leon. If any *federale* recognized him, not one was about to act upon such recognition, knowing the price that was apt to be paid for such ephemeral heroics. Therefore, Juan Guandaro roamed freely through the streets. He reached Avenida Missione unmolested and fumed with anger and rage when he heard of the aborted ambush at the courtyard.

"Heads will roll!" Guandaro seethed. "Heads will roll for this. And if my brother dies..." His voice trailed off, unable to express a vile enough retribution.

Tomas Guandaro was only nineteen, nine years younger and more than seventy pounds lighter than his brother, and when Juan reached his bedside, his life was draining from the bullet wound in his chest. He lay on a dirty pallet just inside the doorway where he had been shot. Dangling from the ceiling overhead, a single naked sixty-watt bulb, threw light on him while a doctor attempted to stanch the flow of blood. Seeing his brother, Tomas forced a weak smile.

"I'll be all right, Juan," he whispered.

"Tomas, Tomas." Guandaro dropped to his knees beside the doctor. He stroked his brother's perspiring forehead, feeling the fire inside the younger man's skull. "Who did this to you?"

"Leave him alone," the doctor advised. "He needs all his strength."

"Who did this to you?" Guandaro repeated, ignoring the doctor.

Tomas licked his lips and tried to speak. A cough rattled up from his congested lungs and blood trickled down the corner of his mouth. He clutched his brother's hand briefly, then let go. His arm dropped limply to his side, and although his eyes remained open there was no life left in Tomas's gaze.

"Tomas, no!" Guandaro shouted. "No! You must live!"

The doctor checked Tomas's pulse and sighed wearily, shaking his head. "He is gone, Sergeant."

With a piercing glare, Guandaro silenced the doctor, then motioned for him to leave. Alone with Tomas, Guandaro hoisted the dead youth and cradled him in his massive arms. In the fourteen years in which Juan Guandaro had risen from an underage military recruit to become the head of San Leon's secret police, he had heard more than his share of profane euphemisms, and during the next few minutes he unleashed the most repugnant of those expressions, cursing through his tears, swearing vows of vengeance.

Finally, Guandaro composed himself and went to the main room of the abandoned factory. Rust and cobwebs had claimed most of the run-down equipment. In a far corner two men stood over a battered figure, who was tied to a chair beneath a mechanical arm that had once been used to transfer completed products from the assembly line to a waiting truck. On cue from the man beside him, the taller officer swung the metallic arm on its ball-bearing swivel, striking the captive in the chair.

David Keliersa screamed as the blow sent shock waves through his already tormented body. His bullet wound had proved less serious than Tomas's, but each time he was jarred by the brutal force of the machine arm, he almost wished that he was dead.

"Talk!" the men above him demanded.

"Go to hell," Keliersa moaned, bracing himself for the next blow.

The interrogators were about to strike the prisoner again when Guandaro intervened, telling the taller man, "Leave him to me, Miguel."

Miguel, whose muscular forearms were adorned with tattoos of helmeted skeletons, stepped to one side, limping slightly, and motioned for the other man to move away as well. Guandaro took their place and stood before Keliersa, waiting for the man to look up.

"I recognize you, Keliersa! The big freedom singer, yes? All those songs denouncing El Chocomil and the memory of Marcos Pabro..."

Keliersa made no reply but Guandaro didn't need one. He suddenly burst into motion, grabbing the prisoner with his thick, powerful arms and lifting him, chair and all, then flinging him into the cinder-block wall behind him. The chair broke from the force of the impact and Keliersa landed hard on the cement floor, feeling the knife-sharp pain of broken ribs.

Grabbing the man by the hair, Guandaro jerked Keliersa to a sitting position and held his head in place as he leaned over so that they were facing, eyeball to eyeball.

Guandaro spit in Keliersa's face. "Before I am finished with you, you will learn another kind of singing...."

1

Fall was still weeks away, but already there were hints of the change in seasons throughout Virginia's Shenandoah Valley. The morning air had that crisp bite that clouded one's breath, and leaves on the deciduous trees were beginning to change color. Nearing the end of his postdawn jog around the perimeter of Stony Man Farm, Jack Grimaldi noticed a bank of dark clouds lumbering eastward across the Blue Ridge Mountains. Cold rain coming, the strapping six-footer mused, slowing to a walk. Something about days like this filled him with an almost melancholic nostalgia. It brought back memories of his teen years in Baltimore, when cold, wet autumn mornings signaled the beginning of school and football season and romantic pursuits involving hayrides and bonfire pep rallies. It astonished him how naive he had been back then, blissfully unaware of the world beyond the cozy confines of his suburban neighborhood. He thought for a moment how nice it would be to have another crack at that uncomplicated life, unspoiled by the harsh realities of death, war and corruption.

Ah, Jack, but you can't go home again, he sighed to himself as he headed across the grounds to the cluster of inconspicuous-looking farm buildings that housed one of the nation's best-kept and most vital secrets. With his parents long in their graves and the two-story brownstone he grew up in long-since demolished to make way for a shopping plaza, this complex was actually the closest thing Grimaldi had now to a home. As a crack pilot capable of handling virtually any sort of aircraft, Jack was in constant demand by Stony Man One, Mack Bolan, and the men of Able Team and Phoenix Force, the two shit-kicking hellsquads charged with tackling the nation's more secretive and dangerous missions against enemies at home and abroad. Between stints in the cockpit, Jack spent most of his free time here, tending to the small jets and choppers kept at the farm's remote airfield or killing time with those same men he risked his life with on the field of battle.

Lately, there'd been little spare time to be killed, and Grimaldi felt played out and tired by four straight months of action. He knew that a few days of R and R would do wonders for his psyche and the myriad aches and pains he'd accumulated from his time in the field. Stony Man chief of operations, Hal Brognola, had noticed Grimaldi's fatigue and ordered him to take a week off, starting tomorrow. Jack hadn't put up any of his usual resistance to such an order.

As he headed toward the main farmhouse, Jack looked forward to a nice hot shower and a change into leisure clothes for a quick jaunt to Nashville. A long-time country music enthusiast, he'd been to the Tennessee capital countless times. He knew dozens of watering holes featuring some fine bar bands made up of ace studio musicians eager to cut loose with their best licks in an informal atmosphere. A week of that, along with a steady diet of hush puppies, baked squash and catfish, and he'd return a revitalized man.

"Yo, Mr. G!"

Grimaldi glanced to his right and saw Pol Blancanales waving to him from a clearing fifty yards away. The wiry, white-haired Hispanic was standing with fellow Able Team members Carl Lyons and Gadgets Schwarz, and they were looking at a blueprint Blancanales was holding.

"What's up?" Jack asked as he approached.

"Found this in the communications room," Lyons said, pointing to the blueprint. He was the tallest and the heaviest of the trio. Not that Blancanales and Schwarz weren't built solidly enough to withstand the rigors of life in the blast lane. Grimaldi felt that any one of them could go one-on-one with another and fight to a stalemate. He'd seen enough rough-and-tumble training scraps between them to know.

"Looks like plans for a barn," Jack said, glancing over the paper. "What about it?"

"Look a little closer," Blancanales encouraged. "This isn't your basic 4-H layout."

Indeed, upon closer inspection, Grimaldi realized that although the barn's exterior facade was quite traditional, inside was another story. There were plans for a pair of racquetball courts, weight room, small swimming pool, indoor running track and shower facilities that included a Jacuzzi and whirlpool. The only actual farm facility, situated in a corner, was three horse stables.

"I'll be," Jack murmured. He looked at the others. "So what's the punch line?"

Blancanales pointed to the bottom corner of the blueprint, which spelled out the intended location of the building. "This place is gonna be for us!"

"You're kidding," Grimaldi said. "If that's the case, why's this the first I heard about it?"

"Probably was going to be a surprise," Schwarz speculated, running the edge of his thumb along his trimmed mustache. "Christmas present from Congress."

"Yeah, right," Lyons deadpanned. "That'll be the fucking day. Hell, if those bastards even knew about us, the only thing we'd get for Christmas would be a seat in the hearing room and a few weeks of the third degree."

Lyons was exaggerating only slightly, if at all. The entire Stony Man operation was, of necessity, primarily a covert one, deliberately operating out of the limelight and avoiding as much scrutiny as possible, for the simple reason that its effectiveness depended upon maximum secrecy and unrestrained maneuverability. Having to play "Mother May I" with Congress prior to taking on a terrorist threat or shutting down a major drug operation would serve only to increase the odds against success by giving the enemy fair notice that they were targeted. This need for secrecy kept much of America from knowing the identities of its unsung heroes. When the Stony Man operation was brought into being, great care had been taken to ensure that the men of Able Team and Phoenix Force were not prima donnas eager for celebrity trappings, but rather men of strength and conviction who would be content knowing they had done their jobs well, despite occasional criticism from poorly informed outsiders.

A door opened and a man in an electric wheelchair rolled out onto the front porch of the main house near the four men. Aaron Churchman, paralyzed from the waist down during a siege that had occurred on these grounds several years before, shook his head disapprovingly. "Those plans were for Brognola's eyes and mine only, gents."

"Shouldn't have left them lying out, then, Bear," Blancanales said. "Lead us not into temptation...."

"The chief wants to see you down in the War Room," Churchman countered. "Now."

"Oh boy," Lyons groused. "We gonna get sent to bed without supper?"

Kurtzman took the blueprint and chuckled, "If the meat loaf tastes as bad as it smells, you'll be lucky if you are."

As the men filed past Kurtzman and entered the main house, Grimaldi patted Schwarz on the shoulder and told his cohorts, "Good luck, guys."

"Hey, you're coming in with us, aren't you?"

Grimaldi shook his head. "Sorry, but I got a plane to catch. Nashville's callin'. Thank God I'm a country boy."

Jack bounded up stairs to the second floor while Able Team descended to the basement and passed through a coded access doorway into the War Room, easily the largest chamber in the house. The War Room was used primarily for strategy sessions. The walls were filled with maps charting global hot spots, and lined with file cabinets containing high-level government communiqués and correspondence that Kurtzman had monitored via computer. In the middle of the room was a conference table, where a gray-haired man chewed on a Honduran cigar as he studied a pile of computer printouts.

"Morning, boys," Hal Brognola told the trio. "Sit down, take a load off."

All three men on Able Team were pushing forty and only tolerated being called "boys" by Brognola, who over the years had assumed an almost paternal relationship with them. Also, when he called them "boys" it was usually an indication that he was in a good mood...or that he was buttering them up for some bad news.

"Well, what's it this time, Chief?" Lyons asked as he plopped into one of the government-issue chairs and propped his feet on the edge of the table. He wasn't going to mention the blueprints until Brognola did, and neither were Schwarz or Blancanales.

Brognola set aside the papers and removed the cigar from his mouth, then with a stretch he leaned back in his chair. The Fed looked like a man who'd been putting in too much time behind a desk. There were lines of strain around his mouth and eyes. "I just got a call from the President," he told Able Team. "He has a very interesting proposition for us."

"Let me guess," Lyons said. "He wants us to take out Senator Dwyer and his whole subcommittee before they come up with any more dirt on his Central America policy."

Brognola laughed. "I'm sure he's been tempted to do that, but I think he's looking for something a little more subtle on that front. No, what the President wants—" and here the older man paused to increase the suspense "—is for you three to try to kill him."

Lyons traded glances with Schwarz and Blancanales, nodding toward Brognola. "Did he say what I think he said?"

Schwarz nodded. "Afraid so."

"You had a little locoweed rolled up in that cigar, Chief?" Blancanales wondered aloud.

Brognola said, "Look, it's all pretty cut-and-dried when you get down to it."

"Oh, of course," Lyons deadpanned. "We'll go to Washington, see the sights, ride the Metro, take in a Redskins game, then take out the President on our way to dinner."

"Spare me the shtick for once, would you, Carl?" Brognola stared down the hotheaded blonde, and Lyons finally gave his boss an emphatic please-do-continue nod. The chief tapped his fingers on a flat ceramic tray beside his files. "I'm sure you remember how the Secret Service was planning a major revamp of its protection detail after that near-hit those Iranians pulled off when the President was on vacation. Well, supposedly the improvements have been made and they're looking for a way to test the new security without having to wait for the next pack of kooks to oblige them. The President thought of you guys.''

"How flattering," Blancanales said. "Maybe we should change our name to Able Kooks.''

"I just buttoned Ironman's lip, Pol," Brognola rejoined. "Cut me some slack. Okay?"

Blancanales snapped off a salute. "You're the boss.''

"Look," Brognola went on, "the way the President figures it, if you guys stage an attempted assassination but can't get past the Service, then he can rest assured that any legitimate attempt on his life won't get far, either.''

"Now, that *is* flattering," Schwarz admitted.

"And it also sounds like the biggest goddamn waste of time I can think of," Lyons suddenly cried out, thumping his fist on the table. "Shit, there's enough real threats out there to be tended to without us getting ourselves tied up playing some kind of glorified game of tag with the Secret Service.''

"It's far more than a game and you know it, Carl."

Lyons held his ground. "Damn it, as far as the way we operate is concerned, it *is* a game. We go out there, we're playing for keeps because our lives are on the line, and we know that one wrong move could cash in our chips. That's real. This simulated shit just doesn't cut it. The Service wants some pros to practice against? Fine, let 'em hire some SWAT people looking to put in a little overtime.''

"Come on, come on," Brognola said. "You guys go through simulation exercises all the time. Don't give me grief on this, okay?''

"Forget it." Lyons shook his head and held one fist out, thumb down. Schwarz offered a similar gesture.

"Yeah, Chief," Blancanales said, striking the more diplomatic tone that had long ago earned him the nickname Politician. "We're itching for action. Why can't you put us somewhere where we get to bust some heads?''

Brognola rose from his chair and paced along the far wall, shoulders hunched, brow furrowed. He deliberately avoided facing the others, letting a few seconds of silence well up as a buffer between them.

"Of course," he finally said, "you realize I could just order you to do this and that would be that. But then morale might be a problem, and we don't want that, do we?''

"Gee, no sir," Lyons said in a high schoolboy voice.

"Suppose I dangle a carrot in front of you?''

"What kind of carrot?''

When Brognola turned to face his men, he was grinning. "I couldn't help but notice that you guys managed to get a look at a certain blueprint upstairs.''

Gadgets groaned. "Oh oh, here it comes.''

Still smiling, Brognola sat down. "You see, on the side I've made a little wager with my old friend Rabters at the Service. He doesn't think my men can get past his men and hit the President. I bet him you could.''

"The barn," Lyons guessed. "You bet the barn."

Brognola nodded. "It's a very simple wager. If you guys succeed, the necessary juggling will be done to free funds to build a gymnasium out here. Lord knows you guys have been harping for one long enough."

"And if we don't succeed?"

"Then the money goes to spiff up the Secret Service facilities in Beltsville."

Lyons, Blancanales and Schwarz huddled briefly, then turned to Brognola and offered three thumbs up. "Okay, Chief," Blancanales said. "We'll go for it."

"Good, good," Brognola responded. "Then you'd best get cracking. Time's awasting."

"How's that?" Lyons asked.

"Oh," Brognola said, almost as an afterthought. "I forgot to tell you. You have only twenty-four hours to work with. That was part of the bet."

2

As he watched the most exotic half-clad showgirls in all Rio de Janeiro strut across a nightclub stage festooned with sequins, tinsel and false smoke from hidden blocks of dry ice, Sergei Karanov idly twirled the little umbrella that had come with his zombie. He'd already finished the drink, his second since supper, and he was feeling a little light-headed.

And bored.

It was more than two months since Karanov had left the espionage world that had been his life, and his seclusion had become increasingly unnerving in recent weeks. He had no doubt that both the KGB and the CIA had a price on his head as a result of his part in the recent rise and fall of a San Diego-based religious cult that had been performing mind control experiments on its disciples. The thrills of life as a fugitive, however, differed greatly from those of a Soviet agent, which he had been for thirty years. Once one has been the hunter, it just does not do to be the hunted, he was fond of saying.

The biggest source of consolation during his exile had been the change in his appearance. With tanned skin, shaved head and a leaner physique earned through a disciplined conditioning regime, he looked and felt more fit than he had in years. But there was no cosmetic way to mask his restlessness, his yearning for power and control. He knew that if he didn't take some sort of action soon his anxiety would over-whelm him.

As the music faded and the last stage number of the evening concluded, the long-limbed dancers froze in position. The club's patrons applauded. All the ta-bles and booths in the dimly lit main showroom were filled. Like the stage show, the nightclub itself exuded a certain glitz and glamour, as though it was in Las Vegas. Karanov preferred this club because it was in the hotel where he'd been staying for the past two weeks and where he had firmly established himself under a new identity, John Richniel, a liquor sales-man based in Dallas, Texas. For someone born and raised in Moscow, he had a remarkably convincing Texan accent, and prided himself on his ability to sustain the charade. Just the other night he had man-aged to bluff his way through a forty-minute conver-sation with a Dallas native on vacation in Rio with his wife, and had even charmed the woman enough for her to proposition him during their token turn on the dance floor. Karanov had turned down the offer. He was ready for a woman, but under decidedly different circumstances.

As the stage curtain closed and recorded Hispanic music began to pulsate throughout the club, Karanov reached into the pocket of his Armani suit and with-drew a money clip holding a stack of folded fifty-dollar bills. All week he'd had a chance to study the solicitation procedures at the club. When he handed a waiter two of the bills along with a handwritten note, he knew that he had only a short wait until a bottle of chilled, vintage Château Langoa-Barton would be brought to his table and he would be joined by one of the dancers he'd seen on stage.

As he waited, Karanov donned a pair of tinted glasses and nonchalantly scanned the faces in the club. He had deliberately chosen a table near the back exit, where he could view anyone entering long before he himself would be spotted. Thus far, the precaution had been unnecessary, but tonight the Russian had to catch his breath for a moment, thinking he had spotted an acquaintance from his Central America days. The other man, tall and broad-shouldered, poked his head into the club for only a moment, however, then left without so much as ordering a drink. Noting that the man limped on his way out, Karanov decided he had been mistaken.

A moment later, a tall thin woman in a revealing beige silk dress slithered seductively into the chair across from him. She had glittering beads woven into strands of her blond hair, and her long fingernails were subtly painted to match the deep blue of her eyes.

"You have been watching me for several nights," she whispered in a husky, sultry voice with the faintest hint of a French accent. She smiled and held a crystal glass out for him to fill. "And now I have a chance to watch you."

"Poetic justice, darlin'," Karanov drawled, filling her glass and his own. He made no effort to keep his gaze from taking in the curvature of her breasts beneath the thin fabric of her dress. "And I gotta say, I like what I'm seein' up close, too."

"I'm glad." She sipped her wine and smiled with satisfaction. "You have excellent tastes, *monsieur*...."

"Richniel," Karanov told her with a laugh. "Rhymes with rich-as-hell."

"And are you?"

"Rich as hell? You bet, darlin'." Karanov took a long draw on his wine, then gently dabbed his lips and winked at the woman. "How about if I take you up to my room and show you my portfolio? Who knows, maybe you can do a little shareholdin' before the night's through."

"I think I would like to hold more than a share," the woman responded.

"Mercy!" Karanov feigned astonishment. "You got a dirty mind, darlin'. I like that."

"I'm glad."

"Well, then..." Karanov stood up and plucked the bottle of wine from the standing ice bucket. "Let's head up to the ranch!"

The "ranch" turned out to be Karanov's well-appointed suite on the nineteenth floor, with an unobstructed view of Rio's famed harbor, which winked in the night with lights from boats plying the calm waters. As the woman stood near the window to admire the scenery, Karanov filled another two glasses with the last of the wine, then brought them over for a toast.

"To *amor*," Karanov suggested.

"This is not love, *monsieur*," the woman said with a sad expression.

"Oh no. Don't go breakin' my heart, darlin'."

"This is not love," the woman repeated, smirking as she clinked her glass against the Russian's. "It is *lust*. Let us drink to lust!"

"By all means. To lust!" Karanov sipped his drink, then stepped back and sat on the edge of the bed, looking up at the woman. "How about if we start with you doin' a little of your dancin' just for me?"

"As you wish, John Rich as Hell."

There was a radio built into the room's color television, and once she'd tuned in to a soft jazz station, the woman set down her wineglass and began to undulate, letting her limbs bend in time to the music. Karanov watched her with calm anticipation. His arousal cut through the fog-headed influence of the alcohol, and he grinned with encouragement. *Yes, my love, dance for me, shed your clothes and rub against me. Come close, close, until I can get my hands around your neck.*

She would not be the first to die to suit Karanov's pleasure. He had killed two women in San Diego before his flight to Rio, and before that there had been others. He had killed countless men in the line of duty, but that was another matter. If he snuffed the life of a woman, even as part of a mission, it was seldom an end so much as the last bit of foreplay preceding his special brand of lovemaking.

Tonight, upon finishing with this dancer, he would leave her here and check out of the hotel. He was through with Rio and planned to move on, perhaps to Switzerland or South Africa. Someplace where he could relish the change in scenery and figure out what to do with his life.

A knock on the door suddenly interrupted the woman's salacious performance.

"Damnation!" the Russian cursed. He shouted at the door, "Go away!"

There was another knock, then a plain white envelope slid beneath the door into the room.

The woman continued to dance, trying to reweave the spell she thought she had cast over Karanov. He rose from the bed and angrily snatched up the envelope, ripping it open to read its contents. There were only a few words on a small slip of paper, but they were sufficient to change Karanov's mood drastically and immediately.

"Problem, hmmm?" the woman cooed as she continued to dance close to Karanov, giving off the tantalizing scent of her perfume when she moved. She was just beginning to peel off her dress.

Karanov turned off the radio, then peeled two fifties from his money clip and slipped them between the woman's breasts. "Party's over, darlin'. Beat it, I got business to tend to."

ACROSS THE STREET from his hotel, Karanov entered a run-down tourist trap called the Yanqui Doodle. A tavern specializing in American beers and food, the Doodle was shabbily decorated with cheap, dust-covered knickknacks and old movie posters. The place was nearly empty. Three overweight middle-aged men, wearing nearly identical loud shirts, kept their wives half-shielded in the far corner, as if trying to protect them from five T-shirted, pool-shooting local youths who kept sneaking glances their way and sniggering to one another in Spanish. A bearded bartender washed beer mugs as he humored a drunken old man, who looked as if his elbows were nailed to the counter to keep him from falling to the sawdust-covered floor. Karanov ordered a draft and carried it to an anti-quated Wurlitzer playing an old love song by Bobby Vinton. Sitting next to the jukebox was the same tall man Karanov had spotted earlier at the nightclub.

"*Buenas noches*, Miguel. It has been a while, yes?"

"Four years is not so long, Sergei."

Neither man offered his hand to the other. Karanov sat across from the tall man, noting the tattoos on his forearms. "A bone man on the left arm, too, now."

"The other one was lonely," Miguel said.

"And you have a limp now, too."

"*Sí.*" Miguel grinned and slapped his thigh, boast-ing, "Souvenir from a jealous husband."

Karanov sipped his beer in the silence between rec-ords. Edwin Starr's 'Twenty-Five Miles' crackled soulfully over the speakers, and two of the youths at the pool table started to sing in sync with the song, using cues for microphones.

"How did you find me?" Karanov finally asked Miguel. "And why?"

"You are very popular these days, Sergei," the tattooed man answered cryptically. "There are many people who want you."

"Want me dead."

"True." Miguel reached into his shirt pocket for a pack of Pall Malls and tapped out a cigarette, making a slow ritual out of lighting it. "In fact, at the airport I believe I saw Robert Treblen. He is still KGB, yes?"

Karanov nodded, trying not to show his unease. Treblen handled wet work—dealings in death, particularly for Soviet agents who had betrayed their superiors. If he was in Rio, it was for only one reason.

"Do you know where he is now?"

Miguel grinned again and nodded. "He is feeding the fishes...from the bottom of the bay."

"You killed him?"

"Let's say he had an accident."

Karanov began to sweat. "If KGB finds out he is missing, they will send *two* men after me."

"Then perhaps you should let us help you," Miguel said. "Sergeant Guandaro would like to see you in San Leon. I can get you there tonight."

"How do I know KGB is not paying you to trap me?"

"You don't, Sergei." Miguel flicked ash from his cigarette onto the floor, then glanced lazily back at the fugitive Russian. "You don't have to come. You can leave right now, and keep running."

Karanov downed his beer, weighing his options. He decided he had no options.

"Does Guandaro have an assignment for me?" he asked.

"Yes, and he will explain it to you in person," Miguel said. He grinned again. "I listened outside your room before I left the note. Your Texan accent is still excellent. I can tell you that will come in handy."

"You interrupted a very important meeting," Karanov protested.

"And I saved that young girl's life, too," Miguel countered evenly. "You really must do something about these urges, Sergei. They will prove your undoing if you are not careful."

Karanov wanted to ask Miguel how he knew of the murders, but decided against it. It was already clear that the San Leonian had him over a barrel, and Karanov didn't want to dwell on the realities of his position any more than necessary. He finished his beer and stood up.

"I'll be ready to leave in an hour," he told the man with the tattooed arms.

3

Adjacent to the Tennessee state capitol building was a small, enclosed park surrounded on three sides by tall shrubs. In the middle of the lawn was an impressive statue of Andrew Jackson astride a regal stallion, outfitted in the uniform he wore in the Battle of New Orleans in 1815. Across from the statue, three men were sitting on a stone bench. One was Brian Darling, looking haggard and pale despite attempts to make himself as presentable as possible. Next to him was Frank Hirsh, head of the Nashville chapter of the Crusade for Conscience. The two of them had spent close to an hour talking with their congressman, Gus Will, an ex-TSU football standout with red hair and a thin mustache covering most of a hereditary harelip. Will listened intently to the CFC's allegations regarding the activities of San Leon's El Chocomil del Sangre, particularly Darling's recollection of his brush with death on Avenida Missione several days before. Occasionally he scribbled a few notes on a legal pad propped on his lap.

"Gentlemen, this is certainly a convincing picture you paint of secret police activity," the congressman conceded after Darling had finished his remarks. "But

I'm sure you realize that the bulk of your information is either hearsay or circumstantial."

"We have the sworn testimony of eleven San Leonians who've witnessed forced incarcerations," Hirsh repeated emphatically, pounding his fist in his open palm. "And Brian here nearly died from his run-in with El Chocomil. That alone should be cause enough for an official investigation."

Will skimmed over his notes and let out a slow sigh. He regarded Brian with a look of patient indulgence, like a prosecuting attorney building up to the key moment in his cross-examination. "Tell me, Mr. Darling...did these men who confronted you ever identify themselves as members of El Chocomil?"

"Of course they didn't!" Brian snapped. "They're the *secret* police, for Christ's sake! Can't you figure out—"

"Easy, Brian, easy," Hirsh interjected, touching his hand.

"Look, I appreciate what you went through and I hate having to play devil's advocate," Will told the younger man, "but I'm just trying to give you an idea of what you're up against if you try to pursue this without any hard documentation."

"Like a bullet in my back?" Brian exclaimed, raising his voice. Several capitol employees lunching in the park glanced at the three men.

"Mr. Darling," the congressman said. "Face facts. We both know that there's going to be no admissions from anyone of position in San Leon on this incident. If anything, they'll raise a stink about your being away from the base without proper papers or authorization. And this contact of yours, David Keliersa...he hasn't been back in touch with you since—"

"Because they probably killed him, you moron!" Brian raged, fed up with Will's patronizing.

"Brian," Hirsh said, "please try to control yourself."

"Oh, fuck it, what's the use?" Brian railed on. "A congressional investigation will help us get the evidence we need to shut El Chocomil down, but they're so goddamn chicken shit they won't move an inch until we bring in a smoking gun with somebody's finger still on the trigger. It doesn't make sense!"

"Okay, that does it," Congressman Will said, closing his notepad and standing up. "You both have my sympathies, but obviously you don't understand the situation from my side, so we're wasting each other's time."

"Wait," Hirsh said, standing up with Will. "Let me—"

"Good day, Mr. Hirsh, Mr. Darling."

Will turned and bounded up the stone steps leading back to the capitol building. Hirsh watched him go, then turned and saw Brian striding off in the opposite direction. He hurried to catch up.

"Slow down, Bri—"

"The hell with it, **Frank**," Brian said without breaking his stride. Together they took the long, steep flight of steps leading down from the capitol's knoll and proceeded along the street to a parking lot near the old Municipal Auditorium.

"You can't give up, Brian."

"Watch me." The men had come in separate cars. As he unlocked his '73 Nova, Brian told his associate, "I'm quitting CFC, as of now."

"No."

"Yes, Frank."

"But this is just a minor setback."

Brian shook his head, slid in behind the wheel, rolled down the window and looked up at Frank. "You don't get it, do you?"

"Get what?"

"Frank, I shot two men down there. Maybe even killed them. What does that make me besides one of them?"

"You were protecting yourself."

"I used violence, and CFC is opposed to violence. I can't belong anymore."

"You've just been under a lot of strain, Brian. Don't do this so rashly. Give it some thought."

Brian started the engine. "Hell, it's all I've been thinking about since I got on the plane to come back. I tried to play along like nothing happened, but it just won't wash. And having to put up with politicians like Will only makes things worse. I can't handle it."

Seeing that argument was useless, Hirsh stepped back from Brian's car, nodding. "Okay, Brian," he said. "Do what you feel you have to. But at least stay in touch, all right? I care about what happens."

"Thanks."

Brian left the lot and headed down to Broadway. His knuckles were white on the steering wheel and he felt his stomach tightening with knots. He hadn't had more than a few hours of sleep per night since his return from San Leon, and even those few hours had been marred by nightmares involving the shooting of David Keliersa and being threatened with a gun. For so long he had lived a life removed from violence. He had seen it in photographs, read about it in the papers, heard about it from victims. Now he knew of it firsthand. He'd faced violence and responded in kind. Etched in his mind even more indelibly than the incident in the courtyard was the sight of the man in the street falling to one side after Brian had shot him. Even though it had been dark, Brian had a vivid impression of the man's face, his look of incredulity and sudden pain.

He drove along Broadway until it became West End Avenue. Near Centennial Park, with its life-size replica of the Greek Parthenon, Brian turned onto a side street and parked in the carport behind his apartment building.

Still lost in thought, he automatically retrieved his mail from the rows of boxes in the ground floor hallway, then headed upstairs to the second story. It was only after his key was in the lock and he was opening his door that he was roused from his thoughts by an intuition that something was wrong.

There was someone inside his apartment.

El Chocomil, he thought to himself in a flash of terror. A death squad from San Leon had tracked him down to finish the job. Weak in the knees, he was too paralyzed by fear either to flee or even to close the door.

"Happy Birthday!"

It was his sister.

Roxanne, smiling at her brother, stood in the middle of the apartment, holding a two-tiered cake smothered with chocolate frosting and topped with candles.

"Surprised?"

Brian nodded feebly as he closed the door behind him. Once his pulse was back under control, he mustered a smile and told Roxanne, "Thanks for remembering."

"You didn't think I'd forget, did you?" she said, putting the cake on a small oak table in the corner of the efficiency apartment. The room, sparsely furnished, was filled mostly with books.

"I also have spaghetti cooking, brother dearest, so why don't you have yourself a drink and sit down."

Brian shook his head with disbelief and gave Roxanne a grateful hug. "Boy, you don't know how much I needed this, sis."

"Oh, yes I do," Roxanne responded, breaking away from Brian to turn down the flame on the stove. "You've been down in the dumps ever since we got back from the tour."

"I know," he said.

"Can't you tell me what's wrong? I don't mean to pry but, Brian, I know you. It has something to do with when you sneaked away from the base. You went into town to see something besides the festivities, didn't you?''

Torn with indecision, Brian looked at his sister. When she had finally agreed to let him accompany her on the USO trip to San Leon, he hadn't mentioned anything about his ulterior motive. Why worry her needlessly, and perhaps even drag her into a dangerous situation? He went to the refrigerator and helped himself to a beer. As he opened it, he smiled and told Roxanne, ''Let's forget about that, okay? This is my birthday, so let's just have a good time.''

4

The rules were simple.

Able Team had to act as if it were a foreign hit team blowing into D.C. with the expressed intention of killing the President. As such, its members couldn't request any favors through the "old boy network" to make their job easier. However, since there was a possibility that an assassination team might have a mole inside the United States intelligence network, they weren't prohibited from trying to make new contacts or otherwise to secure classified information that might be available to enemy forces with the right resources and abilities. And they had until eleven o'clock the following morning to carry out their hit.

It took them several hours to round up the special equipment and weapons they felt would be needed for this most bizarre of assignments. By the time they arrived in Washington in a rented Chevy Beretta, rush-hour traffic was choking the thoroughfares. They circled around the capitol and finally exited Interstate 1 near North Brentwood in Maryland, a short drive from the District of Columbia border. There they checked into the Attaché, a plush but nondescript hotel situated close to the northwest branch of the

Anacostia River. The hotel had been chosen primarily because of its strategic location, being nearly equidistant from the nation's primary intelligence nerve centers—Maryland's Fort Meade and Beltsville, bases for the National Security Agency and Secret Service; the FBI's Hoover Building near Capitol Hill; the CIA's headquarters in Langley, Virginia; and the Pentagon's facilities in Arlington.

They booked into a thirteenth-floor penthouse suite that faced the nation's capitol, barely visible beyond the rise of Bunker Hill and dense suburbs crowded with D.C.'s ever-increasing population. Within moments after taking their luggage up to the suite, the men slipped into a nearby stairwell. Blancanales and Lyons stood watch over the corridor while Schwarz stole up to the roof and attached a small transmitting/receiving device to the large satellite dish used by the hotel to pull in cable television signals for its guests. He attached a thin fiber-optic cable to the mounted device, unrolled it to the edge of the roof, then lowered the unwinding spool to the terrace of their suite. This task accomplished, Schwarz paused a moment to watch the setting sun seemingly impale itself upon the tip of the distant Washington Monument. The storm front that had been advancing on Stony Man Farm almost twelve hours before was now far off on the horizon, filling the sky with vibrant colors.

"So far, so good," Gadgets told his cohorts once they were back in their room. "Let's just hope everything else goes smoothly."

Although Lyons, Schwarz and Blancanales had packed only one change of clothes each and minimal toiletries, they had brought along three bulging suitcases. Most of the space inside was used for storing the minicomputer and high-tech attachments Gadgets would need to tap through security shields at various government agencies in hopes of ascertaining both the President's personal agenda for the next fourteen hours and the extent of the Secret Service's new protection measures. The intercept system was similar to the larger and more sophisticated computer operation Aaron Kurtzman had assembled back at Stony Man Farm. As Able Team's resident mechanical genius, Schwarz had spent his share of hours at Kurtzman's side, learning the delicate techniques of the microchip trade and helping the Bear devise new ones. All told, Schwarz's expertise in prying into other agency computers almost rivaled that of Kurtzman, and easily surpassed the prowess of the most talented amateur hacker who had ever received media coverage. While most hackers depended upon modems and telephone lines, Schwarz and Kurtzman had evolved supplementary means of computerized infiltration that penetrated farther and were virtually untraceable.

It took Schwarz almost an hour to get his system assembled and hooked up to a special battery pack that in itself filled three-quarters of the largest suitcase. Although the computer was also plugged into the room current, the battery pack assisted in cranking out the high amount of power needed to run the complicated, high-speed monitoring programs. Without the batteries, the hotel management might notice that an excessive amount of electricity was being gobbled up by the folks in suite 13H.

While Schwarz was setting up, Lyons and Blancanales holed themselves up in separate bathrooms with makeup kits, slightly altering their appearance to avoid being recognized by Secret Service or other Washington heavyweights who might have previously seen them in action. When they rejoined Schwarz, both men had darkened their hair and added paste-on mustaches. Blancanales had gone all out and covered his chin with a beard. Inspecting each other, the men broke out laughing.

"Hey, Ironman, I didn't think it was possible for you to get any uglier," Blancanales snickered. "Boy, was I wrong."

"Nobody's going to mistake you for Prince Charming, either, Rugface," Lyons shot back with a grin.

"You'll both pass muster, that's the important thing," Schwarz said after looking them over. As the member of Able Team most often assigned to don disguises, he was in a position to know what he was talking about. "Just be glad it's cooled down the past week so you don't have to worry about losing your mustaches."

"How much time you figure you need, Gadgets?" Lyons asked, gesturing at the computer setup.

"Four hours easy," Schwarz said, reeling in the fiber optic cable from the terrace and linking it with his main microprocessor. ''If there's been any alteration on their comp-guard configurations, it could be a lot longer. You guys might as well head out. Call me sometime around midnight. If I come up with something sooner, I'll beep you.''

''You got it.'' Lyons clipped a palm-size communicator under his sport coat, then turned and draped an arm across Pol's shoulder, guiding him toward the door. ''Okay, Rugface, let's hit it.''

''Call me Rugface one more time, amigo, and you're the one's gonna get hit.''

''Oooh, touchy touchy.''

Lyons and Blancanales kept up their mutual razzing all the way into D.C. It was a diversion from their apprehensions about the task at hand. In the event that Schwarz could neither uncover the Secret Service's new protection measures nor pinpoint the President's movements for the following morning, Pol and Ironman were about to see if they could get at the Chief Executive that evening. They knew he was having a formal dinner at the White House with leaders from CAF, the Central American Federation, after which it was assumed the group would convene in a conference room for informal talks about the instability in the region, particularly San Leon.

Lyons circled the White House twice before the sun had completely set. He was grateful for the glut of tourist traffic that allowed him to inch along without drawing undue attention. Two passes were enough for him and Blancanales to get a rough idea of the security layout. They were already somewhat familiar with standard protective measures from previous assignments and from a glimpse at a few sheets of data Schwarz had been able to coax out of the computers back at Stony Man. As a concession to the peace of mind of Washington's considerable tourist element, care had been taken to downplay the visibility of most supplementary security measures. But the trained eye could pick out the added sentries on the grounds, the reinforced barricades and other inconspicuous measures.

"Looks like they've upped manpower by half for starters," Lyons observed as he made his last pass behind the White House. "And those are infrared scanners they've added to the remotes."

"I think you're right," Blancanales conceded, drumming his fingers on the armrest. "I wouldn't put money on our being able to get to him if he stays in."

"Amen to that." Lyons turned down New York Avenue and wedged the Beretta into a curbside parking space. "With any luck, Gadgets will find us a weak link."

"Be even better if we can come up with something on our own, eh?" Blancanales said. "Show 'em the ol' human element can't be replaced by computers."

"Sure is worth a try. Time's wasting." Lyons checked the dashboard clock. "Hell, we're already down to thirteen hours."

Lyons and Blancanales had left their usual hardware—Government Model Colt .45s—at the hotel. Since Hinckley's botched assassination attempt at the Washington Hilton, security had tightened enough that it would be virtually impossible to get close to the President with a handgun. As Able Team had no real intention of putting a bullet into the chief of state, a different mode of attack was deemed necessary to win the bet. Before leaving the car, Lyons and Pol quickly checked their weapons of choice, telescoping blowguns made of sturdy plastic that could easily pass through a metal detector. When fully extended to their four-foot length, the guns provided chilling accuracy at close range, and even when they were partially collapsed, it was still possible for a practiced blower to nail a softball-size target from twenty feet. Able Team had become acquainted with blowgun warfare during several of their early assignments, and their fascination with the primitive weapon hadn't diminished. Both Lyons and Blancanales felt that if they could get to within ten yards of the President, they could nail him with the ammunition chosen for this particular mission—small pellets filled with a washable red ink that would leave a stinging "wound" on impact.

"I feel like one of those guys who play war games on weekends," Lyons commented as he and Blancanales backtracked toward the White House, passing the Treasury Department.

"Yeah, but they usually play in the woods," Pol said, "and the other team's not toting real firepower."

"True," Lyons admitted. "Plus they're just going after a fucking flag, not the Big Man."

In the few minutes it had taken them to park, a band of protesters had materialized in front of the White

House. They were waving placards demanding that the United States get out of the United Nations and otherwise keep its nose out the business of San Leon and the other countries of Central America. Several wore skeleton heads, and one woman toted a sandwich board reading "CAF GO HOME!!!!" Nearly all of them were shouting derisive chants through the tall wrought-iron fence that surrounded the White House grounds.

"Wonderful," Lyons remarked cynically as he took in the demonstration. "Now there's no way he's gonna come outside."

"Gee, I don't know," Blancanales said. "Could be he'll come out to rap with the people. You know, a little grass roots in actions."

"Sure, Pol, and maybe a UFO will float down to the Mall and let off a load of aliens that look like Jessica Lange in heat."

"Wouldn't that be nice...."

As is usually the case, a small crowd and a share of the Washington press corps soon surrounded the demonstrators. Pol and Lyons wormed through the throng, paying only slight attention to the action on the sidewalk. Their eyes were on the White House, far beyond the range of their blowguns.

"Let's check out the press," Lyons suggested after they'd heard a few minutes of foreign policy discussion from the demonstrators.

"I've already been checking them out," Blancanales said. He reached inside his coat and removed a handful of laminated press badges, all with his photo prominently displayed. The ID tags had been manufactured earlier that month, with him posing in the same facial disguise he now wore. "I don't see anyone from the *Guardian* here," he said as he pulled out the badge claiming he was a correspondent for that national magazine.

Lyons had a similar badge, which he displayed on his lapel as they wandered away from the curiosity seekers and strolled to the row of mobile TV units parked at the scene. Journalists being territorial scoop mongers by nature, it wasn't easy for the men to strike up a conversation, but finally they were befriended by a local cameraman, who was in the process of reloading his minicam at his van.

"Heard anything about the Pres making a statement after he meets the CAF people?" Lyons asked.

"I'm sure he'll make a statement," the burly man replied without taking his eyes off his equipment. "But it won't be to the press, 'cause it won't be printable. Give him until tomorrow and his speech men will have come up with some good one-liners for him."

"He'll use 'em after that breakfast meeting tomorrow, huh? At the Northgate, right?"

"That's not my shift, so I wouldn't know. 'Scuse me, but I got work to do. Maybe I'll be lucky and these freaks'll wig out." The man hoisted the camera back onto his shoulder and clipped a power pack to his waist, then headed off to rejoin the action near the fence. Lyons watched the man, lost in thought.

"What's up, Ironman?" Blancanales asked him. "I can hear your gears grinding."

"Just an idea," Lyons said. "Just an idea...."

TWENTY MILES AWAY, at the Beltsville headquarters of the Secret Service, the night shift was abuzz with conversation, but not about the protection of the President and the First Family, or even about the countless other duties the agency was charged with. Instead, people were talking about the freak accident that had put John Rabters, the Service's ranking administrator, into a nearby hospital earlier that morning. Driving to the office from his home in nearby Berwyn Heights, Rabters had been forced to stop suddenly to avoid a massive pileup on the Washington Expressway, which was wet from a predawn drizzle. The fifty-seven-year-old agent's Chrysler LeBaron had spun out of control and smashed through a concrete center divider, flipping over before slamming to a halt in the oncoming lanes of morning rush-hour traffic. By some miracle the car hadn't struck any other vehicles, but it was totaled. By the time paramedics used their jaws of life to get at him, Rabters was in a coma and suffering from multiple injuries, including internal bleeding that required four hours of surgery to stop.

The accident had happened before Rabters had had a chance to inform anyone at the Service of his bet with Hal Brognola. No one at Beltsville or any other Secret Service outpost was aware that Able Team was in town to make a simulated attempt on the President's life. The secret was Rabters's alone, and his lips were sealed.

"And he's still in a coma," dispatcher Tommi Smith told Mike Aanero, a tall, rugged-looking officer preparing to tackle Hogan's Alley, the Service's on-site practice range, a meticulously recreated city street where targeted silhouettes would pop out unexpectedly, giving an agent only split seconds to bring his gun into firing position and determine whether the target was another gunman or perhaps just an unarmed drunk stumbling out of an alley.

"Tough break," Aanero said, shaking his head as he loaded his service revolver. Recognized as the top marksman in the Service, Aanero maintained his reputation by hitting Hogan's Alley at every available opportunity. Tonight, for example, he was still on the premises even though it was supposed to be his day off.

"How's it feel aiming for the face out there these days?" Tommi asked, referring to the most recent directive from Service Administration.

"It's a smaller target," Aanero said, slipping the gun into his shoulder holster. "But you're not going to find many punks going after the President wearing bulletproof masks. This way, we hit 'em and they stay hit."

Tommi shuddered. "I'd sure hate to catch one in the face."

Aanero laughed savagely, displaying one of the bullets from his speed-loader. "Honey, one of these comes your way, you don't catch it. It puts a hole in your face, scrambles your brain and keeps on going...."

"Please, Mike, I just ate!"

"Sorry, sweetcakes." Aanero left the side building and proceeded to Hogan's Alley, striding with a confident bravado. Once he was cleared to use the range, he started down the middle of the deserted street like a gunslinger looking to add another notch to his pistol. He had a look that said, I pity the first poor fucker that gets in my way.

That first poor fucker turned out to be the silhouette of a sniper that squeaked slightly on its hinges as it pivoted into view on the fire escape platform of a brick building. Aanero reflexively rolled to his right, removing his revolver in the same fluid motion, and firing four quick shots. The silhouette rattled as three bullets ripped through its face and one pierced its neck.

Aanero grinned with satisfaction. He told the perforated target, "You have the right to remain headless...."

At eight the following morning, Aanero was scheduled to join the shift of Secret Service men protecting the President.

5

From a window seat in the slowly revolving Polaris restaurant atop the Hyatt Regency in downtown Nashville, Jack Grimaldi treated himself to a prime rib dinner while enjoying a 360-degree view of the city's famed skyline. He'd arrived in town a few hours earlier, and had already made an obligatory visit to Music Row, where he browsed through souvenir shops and theme stores, tried on some cowboy boots and admired George Jones's assembled collection of rare automobiles. At several of the emporiums he lingered at the record racks, flipping through the albums of Roxanne Darling to see how she'd changed over the years.

Roxanne Darling.

Thirteen years ago, she and Grimaldi had been quite an item. It was during a wild, unfocused period in Jack's life, between his stint as a combat pilot in Vietnam and the run-in with the Mob that had eventually linked him up with Mack Bolan and the Stony Man operations. He'd been quite a hell-raiser then, living with a few of his vet buddies on an old farm in the country an hour's drive west of Baltimore, his hometown. After long days working as a mechanic and gofer at the private airfield formerly owned by his father, Jack and his comrades invariably spent their nights partying. Their favorite hangout had been a country bar called the Rustlers' Roundup. It was one of those notorious saloons where the bar bands often performed behind chicken-wire barricades to keep from being pelted by ashtrays and beer bottles flung by some yahoo who'd had one too many and was looking for a fight.

One night a new band called the Tennessee Ramblers was playing its first gig at the Roundup. Its lead singer, Roxanne Darling, then a timid, undiscovered young talent, had been so terrified of the raunchy catcalls and come-ons from her rowdy audience that halfway through the first set she had taken refuge behind the drummer and sung with her back to the crowd. Despite her fear, she was still able to belt out song after song with an emotional intensity that soon won over most of the patrons.

Particularly Jack Grimaldi.

Smitten by Roxanne, Jack had left the bar between sets and gone running up and down the road outside, trying to sober himself up so he could make a good impression on her when she was through singing for the night. Unfortunately, after the last song, Roxanne went straight to the parking lot and into a car driven by her teenage brother, Brian. She was whisked away before Jack could elbow his way to the nearest exit. The same thing happened the next night, and the night after that.

Jack finally met Roxanne face-to-face on the fourth night, and despite—or perhaps because of—his uncharacteristic bumbling during his introduction, he made a favorable impression on her. They started dating after that, and within a few weeks were seeing each other exclusively. Partially through Grimaldi's contacts with other bars in the area, the Tennessee Ramblers were able to put the Rustlers' Roundup behind them and play in less threatening environments. Between gigs Roxanne and Jack usually got away together, sometimes to take in the Orioles or Colts back in Baltimore, sometimes to go picknicking in the woods near his farm. During picnics Jack would often sit mesmerized as Roxanne sang new songs she was working on. Other times she would listen with equal fascination to his stories of boyhood misadventure in Baltimore and his subsequent stint as an Army pilot in Vietnam, where he'd earned the Airman's Medal, two Purple Hearts, a Commendation Medal and the Theater Ribbon with Unit Citation.

For seven months they were inseparable. Grimaldi received endless grief from his roommates for having fallen so totally for Roxanne, who was being equally discouraged by her manager, who felt that she needed to spend more time cultivating her career and less time gallivanting about with a fly-boy Romeo.

Things finally came to a head the following fall, when Roxanne's band was asked to be the opening act for the Ray Brothers, who were on a tour that would run from Austin, Texas back to her native Nashville. The offer coincided with Jack's proposition that she live with him in a trailer home he figured to set up on his farm so they could spend even more time together. Forced to choose, Roxanne reluctantly opted for the band. She told Jack she wanted them to stay in touch and maybe even get together at some point along the tour, but Grimaldi balked at what he sensed was a halfhearted consolation prize. Deep down he knew that he was always going to run a close second to Roxanne's career, so he broke things off with her during a bitter argument that effectively negated the bliss of the previous months.

While Roxanne went on to lay the groundwork for her later success, Grimaldi let his bitterness get the better of him, and lapsed into self-destructiveness and nihilism. This led to his dark "Mafia period," lasting several years, from which he was eventually rescued by Mack Bolan.

Throughout this time, despite his involvement with dozens of women and a practiced "Teflon response" that supposedly prevented him from being hurt by any romantic intrigue, Jack had still never completely gotten over Roxanne. He had been certain, however, that she had forgotten him, until the first Roxanne Darling album came out. One of the songs was entitled "Rescued from the Roundup" and related Roxanne's gratitude to "a good country boy who smoothed the hard times." Though touched by the sentiment, Grimaldi didn't try to contact her. But all the same, one of the reasons he liked visiting Nashville was because that city had become her permanent

home when she wasn't touring, and so there was a remote chance he would run into her.

Tonight it looked as if Fate might accommodate
him.

Jack had bought a paper on the way to the restaurant, and while sipping an after-dinner coffee he
flipped to the entertainment section. It contained a
small blurb about Roxanne Darling's recent return
from a USO performance for United Nations troops
stationed in San Leon. In its last paragraph, the story
mentioned a rumor that she might drop in to the
Grand Ole Opry that evening to try out a few songs
from her upcoming album.

Grimaldi checked his watch. Forty-five minutes
until showtime. That would have been no problem if
the Opry were still performing out of Ryman Auditorium, only a few blocks away. However, the shows
now emanated from Opryland Amusement Park,
more than ten miles northwest of the city. The new
theater was a large, wood-framed building capable of
seating more than four thousand people.

"Damn!"

Leaving twenty dollars to cover his tab, Grimaldi
hurried to the elevator and rode down to the lobby,
then exited onto Union Street, where he jumped into
his rented Corsair. He made good time crossing the
Cumberland River and getting on the Galatin Pike,
which he took north to Briley Parkway. Although
Jack's forte was winged aircraft, he was no slouch behind the wheel of an automobile. He weaved through
traffic with effortless grace, teasing the speed limit and

several times passing it. His anticipation was building by the second, for he had decided that this time, one way or another, he was going to see Roxanne Darling, if only on stage for a few minutes.

Twenty-eight minutes later, he parked his car in the Opryland lot and was weaving through the crowd entering the park. He reached the head of the ticket line just three minutes before show time, only to discover that his rush had apparently been in vain. "I'm sorry, sir," the woman inside the kiosk informed him, "but we sold out nearly an hour ago."

Grimaldi groaned, unable to hide his disappointment. "Is Roxanne Darling going to be here tonight?" he asked.

"She's not scheduled," the woman said, "but I did hear that she's backstage, so..."

"Thank you," Jack said, turning away from the kiosk and taking his wallet from his pocket. Joining the flow of humanity heading for the entrances of the new Opry, he waved a greenback in the air and shouted, "I'll pay fifty dollars for an orchestra seat!"

In three seconds, four people were at his side with tickets they were willing to sell. He chose the seat closest to the stage and felt another rush of expectation as he entered the Opry House. He had an aisle seat just right of center stage, seven rows back. A warm-up comedian, standing in front of the stage curtains, was finishing his routine with a plug for an Opry-run bus tour that ran daily excursions past the homes of country stars. Once he'd left the stage to sign up a handful of prospective sightseers, the crimson curtains parted and a joyous ovation greeted Lefty Kyle and the Tumbleweeds, who launched into a bluegrass rendition of "The Orange Blossom Special" in front of the red-and-white barn facade that was a longtime trademark of the Grand Ole Opry. Dozens of camera-toting spectators rushed down the aisles and crouched before the stage to snap photos of the country legend, who wore his patent sequin suit and sang with a voice that had lost little power over forty years.

As it had been since 1925, the Opry show was being transmitted live via WSM radio to affiliate stations throughout the land. After the opening number, Lefty Kyle introduced radio announcer Jimmy Davniro, who welcomed the crowd and announced that the first half hour of the show was being sponsored by Murrenfeld's Stock and Feed Supply. A short commercial followed, after which Lefty led his band through a brief medley of his two signature songs, "Sparkle and Shine" and "Lonesome Prairie Boy." Hearing the songs, Jack felt choked up, as they reminded him of his Baltimore childhood when his folks would spend summer nights playing Lefty Kyle records in the backyard.

After the second ovation died down, Kyle thanked the crowd and said, "Since you seem like such nice people, it hardly seems right to keep you in suspense all night long." He grinned as a renewed burst of applause and cheers rumbled through the auditorium, then went on. "Here she is, ladies and gentlemen, everyone's country darlin', Roxanne Darling!"

Roxanne strode out onto the stage, smiling at the din of adulation that greeted her. The Tumbleweeds played backup as she strapped on a guitar and launched into a feisty version of "Thinking about You." Flashbulbs winked throughout the auditorium and fans crushed the front of the stage trying for close-ups. Roxanne accommodated them as best she could, squinting past the stage lights to offer them her winning smile.

Then she saw Jack Grimaldi.

He stood up in his seat and was half a head taller than anyone around him. When their eyes met he nodded and offered her an uncertain smile. Even after all these years, it took only that quick passing glance for her to recognize him. In her surprise she forgot her lyrics. The band kept playing and she regained her composure in time to come in on the next verse.

Embarrassed that he had distracted her, Jack sat down. Was she glad to see him? He found himself wishing he hadn't come, and as he sank lower in his seat, he thought about leaving with the fans who were pulling back from the stage by the end of the song. But he decided to ride it out. After all, there was a chance that she hadn't really recognized him at all.

"Thank you, thank you," Roxanne told her cheering admirers. "It's so good to be back in Nashville!"

This brought on another ovation, and when things calmed down, Roxanne tuned her guitar as she explained. "I was going to do another song from my new album, but I just noticed an old, dear friend in the audience, and there's a song I'd like to dedicate to him.''

She turned to whisper a few words to Lefty Kyle, who passed along cues to the Tumbleweeds. In unison, Roxanne and Lefty harmonized the opening verse of ''Rescued from the Roundup.''

In a backwater bar at the edge of town
Rowdy country boys like to really get down
A chicken-wire fence between them and us.
The louder I sang the louder they cussed.
Oh, Lord, I felt bound up,
And I wanted to be rescued
From the Roundup...

For the next four minutes a chill ran down Jack's spine continuously, as Roxanne sang of their early courtship. He'd heard the song countless times before, but it had never hit him as it was doing now. Biting his lower lip, he had to blink back the dampness creeping across his eyes. Hey, calm down, big guy, he told himself. Get a grip.

Because the Opry's multiguest format restricted each performer to a couple of numbers only, Roxanne bade the crowd farewell after ''Rescued from the Roundup,'' and Mike Robesson valiantly walked out with his pearl-laden banjo to assume the challenge of keeping up the crowd's enthusiasm. He took the safe way out, opting for ''Foggy Mountain Breakdown.''

Grimaldi barely heard Robesson or any other performer after him. His mind was far away, caught up somewhere between the distant past and the uncertain present. It took two nudges for an usher, crouching next to his aisle seat, to get Jack's attention. "Note for you from Ms Darling."

Jack opened the envelope slowly, not sure what he would find inside. It turned out to be a map of the Opry's Nashville bus tour route, with a circle around Roxanne Darling's Oak Park home. She had written directions as well as her home phone number in the margin, along with a quick note:

> What a shock! Jack, is it really you? Sorry, but I had to leave for a studio session. Will you be in town Sunday? I have all morning free. Please? It's been too long.
>
> Love, Roxanne

This was Friday night. Jack had planned on staying in Nashville at least until Tuesday. During the next commercial break, he dialed Roxanne's number on a pay phone in the lobby. As he expected, she had an answering machine. He waited out her recorded message, then left one of his own.

> Hi, Roxanne. It's Jack. I'll be there at eleven on Sunday, okay? I'm staying at the Maxwell House if you need to confirm or change the time. And you're right. It *has* been too long. . . .

6

Four miles north of San Leon City, the myriad cones
of a volcanic belt form a natural national boundary.
Like the capital city, each of the huge mounds was
named for a saint, although deep within their bowels
churned a less-than-heavenly hellfire of glowing lava
and explosive, sulfuric gases, which periodically
emitted warning clouds of smoke. It was more than
fifteen years since an actual eruption, but there were
still grim reminders of that outburst just outside the
city, where the village of Sanishago had been laid
asunder by a juggernaut of churning mud and lava. By
and large, the citizens of San Leon City kept their distance from the ominous peaks, and whenever prayers
were recited, either in the new Christian mission or at
pagan gatherings, there were always fervent supplica-
tions that mounts Patricio, Francisco and Roberto
would not blow their respective tops and bring doom
to the land.

Although the prayers seemed to be working, the
mountains had become the source of another type of
threat to the well-being of San Leonians. For it was
there, more than five thousand feet above the city, that

El Chocomil, the secret police, based its fearful operations.

Under the mantle of night, a weathered Jeep crawled up the narrow, treacherous dirt road that girded Mount Francisco like a lengthy half-healed scar. Miguel was behind the wheel, leaning forward and peering through the bug-flecked windshield. He'd made this trip dozens of times but knew better than to take the blind, winding turns for granted. Boulders dislodged from the slopes above occasionally found their way into the middle of the thoroughfare, and more than once he'd had to brake when confronted by a stray mule or llama that had wandered out of the surrounding brush.

"I thought you would have had this place paved by now," Sergei Karanov, sitting in the passenger seat, said dryly.

"And as soon as we did that tourists buses would be coming up for a look at things."

"I was joking, Miguel," Karanov said. "I haven't forgotten your need for secrecy."

"Good," Miguel called out over the grinding of gears as he put the vehicle into four-wheel drive for the last perilous stretch to the summit. "We will be there soon."

"I hope so." Despite his sarcasm, Karanov was actually enjoying the ride and the prospects of taking on an assignment for El Chocomil. It would mean a return to the offensive, to the kind of life he felt destined for. Ah, to be a hunter again, he thought to himself, breathing in the pungent smell of the tropical growth clinging to the mountainside. And it was good to be in San Leon again. The place was filled with pleasant memories for him, taking him back to a time when he was a KGB field agent, authorized to act alone, to travel light, to stalk and kill if the situation called for it. This was just what his jaded soul needed.

Clearing the top of the mountain, the men proceeded down a straight, gradual slope in the road, rolling past a sight a tourist would not have expected at this elevation. Stretching between Mount Francisco and the higher peaks of mounts Roberto and Patricio was a lake. *El chocomil*, the pernicious wind after which the San Leon secret police had been named, normally blew down from the mountaintops in late afternoon and churned the water into a turbulent maelstrom for many hours. This evening, however, there was only the faintest of breezes, and the lake was nearly as smooth as glass, reflecting the peaks and the overhead slice of moon. *Tul* reeds grew upright like thick green hairs near the shore, and through them Karanov could see a small, high-powered boat floating out on the water.

Two men were standing upright in the craft, holding a sobbing peasant woman between them, whose arms and legs were bound together. In the moonlight Karanov noticed that her legs were also tied to a boulder the size of a small filing cabinet. Oblivious to the woman's weeping, the men were shouting at her, and Karanov's Spanish was adequate enough for him to understand that they were questioning her regarding the whereabouts of her husband.

"She is married to one of our enemies," Miguel explained unnecessarily. "He fired at one of our trucks the other night, injuring two men. We want to know where he's hiding."

"And she's not going to tell you," Karanov surmised.

"That is the last mistake she will make," Miguel said, laughing. His prediction was borne out moments later, as the screaming woman was tossed overboard. Her cries were promptly silenced as the boulder around her ankles pulled her down to the lake's bottom.

"The fish are well fed here," Karanov observed.

"This is true." Miguel chuckled.

Halfway around the lake, Miguel turned off the road and pulled into a large camp nestled in the foothills of Mount Roberto. Several camp fires threw their flickering light on men in the uniforms of El Chocomil, who were smoking cigarettes and drinking chili-spiced coffee as they traded stories of their most recent exploits of terror in the city below. Some were relating the widespread mourning throughout San Leon over the tragic death of folksinger David Keliersa, who had allegedly died in a grisly freak accident in which his car tumbled down a steep ravine near his home and burst into flames. Those of El Chocomil knew it had been no accident, and that Keliersa had been dead long before the secret police had driven his car off the road.

As the Jeep rolled past the hardened men, there were murmurs of "Gaucho," the nickname Karanov had earned for the Western wear he had favored during his first stint in San Leon.

"Nice to be remembered," Karanov said, running his hand over his bald head. "But I don't know how they could recognize me."

"They probably don't, but they do know that it was you I went to fetch for the sergeant," Miguel told him.

The man with the tattooed arms parked the Jeep near the entrance of a large cave, which was blocked by a barred gate. Inside the cavity a small fire burned, allowing Karanov to see about forty emaciated, ragged prisoners crowded together in the dirt. Those with some strength and defiance left in their weary frames shouted curses at Miguel, who returned their taunts and commanded them to be silent. Hearing the oaths continued, he approached the bars and grabbed an Atchisson automatic shotgun from one of the guards. He aimed through the bars and fired two rounds at the ceiling. The explosive blasts reverberated loudly off the cavern's scalloped walls, racking the eardrums of the prisoners, while ricocheting steel balls and fifty No. 2 shot bit randomly into those unfortunate prisoners in the wrong place at the wrong time. Wailing and moaning replaced the cursing. Miguel returned the shotgun to the guard and led Karanov around a cluster of boulders to a large tent nearby. Four shotgun-wielding guards were stationed at each corner of the canvas structure, which glowed eerily from within. From behind it came the dull whine of a muffled power generator.

"Karanov is here," Miguel called out, standing at the entrance to the tent.

"Let him in," came the voice of Juan Guandaro from inside.

Miguel held open the flap and gestured for Karanov to enter. The Russian did so and found himself in surroundings as lavish as the cave had been barren. Somehow Guandaro had managed to haul up the finest plunder from victims of his late-night raids on San Leon City. Priceless carpets lined the floor and plush antique furniture lined the canvas walls. A stereo drowned out the sound of the generator with classical music. Sitting in a stuffed leather chair behind a large teak desk, Juan Guandaro was examining a photo album of country music stars, and in particular a picture of Roxanne Darling.

"Ah, Sergei!" Guandaro intoned, rising to a half-crouch, shaking Karanov's hand, and gesturing to a chair opposite the desk. "Please sit. It's so good to see you, my friend."

Karanov chose instead one of the softer couches across the tent. Guandaro circled around the desk to join him, pausing near a small cooler.

"Refreshment?" he asked the Russian. "I have *cerveza*, wine . . . perhaps some champagne?"

"A beer," Karanov said.

Guandaro opened a chilled bottle and handed it to the Soviet, smiling. "I like this new look of yours, Sergei. Very machismo."

"I doubt that you brought me here to discuss my grooming, Guandaro."

"Juan. You must call me Juan," the sergeant insisted, sitting down with a glass of wine. "Or Chico, yes?"

Karanov had to smile at this reference to his earlier assignment in San Leon, which Guandaro proceeded to recall with the fondness of an alumnus recalling his collegiate pranks at a twenty-year reunion. Four years earlier, Karanov had been sent to San Leon to infiltrate El Norte, a hotel in the capital city popular with the American press and diplomatic corps. Even then, Karanov's uncanny mastery of regional American dialects had been legendary, and he had managed to wangle himself a job in the El Norte cocktail lounge, where he performed country and western songs between one-liners stolen from American television shows. Mustached and dressed in cowboy suits and ten-gallon hats as part of his act, Karanov became known to some members of El Chocomil as Gaucho, while Guandaro had nicknamed him Gaucho Marx. Karanov retaliated by calling the sergeant Chico. And, of course, the punch line was always that their third brother was Karl Marx, who couldn't be in town for obvious reasons.

"And you were so good, Sergei!" Guandaro boasted at the end of his stroll down memory lane. "You had those diplomats and reporters in the palm of your hand! I swear, if you had been allowed to stay on stealing inside stories, we would still be in power now and not forced to slink around like wolves in the night."

"You like to slink around at night," Karanov told Guandaro without malice. "It's your nature."

"You may be right." Guandaro chuckled.

Karanov finished his beer and set it on the coffee table in front of him. "Enough nostalgia, Juan," he said. "Let's talk about the present."

"The present." Almost instantaneously Guandaro's mood turned dark. He rose to his feet and began to pace the tent. "I have a personal favor to ask of you, Sergei. It is no business of the KGB. They do not know I have contacted you. I ask you this favor as Juan Guandaro alone."

"Go on," Karanov told him.

"My brother was killed several days ago by an American," the sergeant explained, returning momentarily to his desk to retrieve the photo book. He showed Karanov the photo of Roxanne Darling. "The killer was her brother. He was with her when she came to sing for the U.N. soldiers near the city. He works for an organization in America that is trying to expose our activities.

"I want him dead, and I want to send a message to this organization to stay out of matters that are not their concern."

Karanov stared impassively at the photo and said nothing for several seconds. Then he looked up at Guandaro and asked, "Why me?"

"Because this Brian Darling lives in Nashville," Guandaro said. "If he is staying with his sister, he may share in the protection she receives as a singing star. I cannot send just anyone to handle this matter. We tried a year ago to send some of our people to the States on a mission. Now they are rotting in a prison there. No, for this job, it should be someone who can mix in with the Americans. You, and maybe some of your contacts in the States.''

Karanov nodded. ''It could be arranged.''

''You can name your fee,'' Guandaro said. ''At any price, the revenge would be worth it.''

Karanov took less than half a minute to decide. ''I'll do it,'' he said.

''Good! I knew I could count on you.''

Karanov pointed at Roxanne Darling's picture. ''Do you want anything done with her? She is very popular in the States, you know.''

Guandaro caught the subtle meaning of Karanov's question. ''And very valuable, yes?''

''Yes.''

''Worth perhaps a handful of our people stuck in American prisons?''

''Perhaps.''

Guandaro smiled. ''I like the way you think, Gaucho.''

''Another beer,'' Karanov suggested, loosening up.

''By all means.'' Guandaro obliged the Russian, then returned to his desk and retrieved a sheet of paper. ''Perhaps this might help you to get to Roxanne Darling.''

Karanov looked at the sheet and frowned. ''A song?''

"Not just any song," Guandaro said. "It was written by David Keliersa. We found it on him before his unfortunate accident."

The Soviet looked over the lyrics, raising an eyebrow. "This song is very critical of El Chocomil."

"Exactly," Guandaro said. "What better bait for those we wish to lure to their doom?"

7

As he did every morning, Aaron Kurtzman began his day with a half hour of stretching exercises and weight training designed to provide a full cardiovascular workout and maintain the muscle tone of his upper body. Though confined to a wheelchair, the Bear saw no reason to forsake a lifelong dedication to fitness, and he prided himself in the feeling of self-reliance the regimen provided. Because of the strength in his forearms and biceps, after his workout he was able to pull himself from his chair and into a customized shower with a built-in stool.

While he was dressing, Kurtzman finally gave in to the curiosity that had been building inside him since the day before. As part of the bet with the Secret Service, Able Team was forced to remain incommunicado with Stony Man Farm during the twenty-four hours covered by the wager. Had the would-be hit on the President taken place? Kurtzman was reliant on the media and his own eavesdropping capabilities to find out. There had been no news by the time he had retired the previous evening. Turning on a morning television news program, he watched for mention of an assassination attempt during the night. Of course,

Able Team might have made the attempt without the media's being witness to it, in which case the American public would most likely never learn of it. In any event, the only news out of Washington concerned the previous evening's demonstration outside the White House. Kurtzman caught a fleeting glimpse of a man who might have been Lyons mingling with the demonstrators, but the camera panned past him and settled on the group's spokesman instead.

Dressed, Kurtzman took the elevator down from his second floor quarters and quickly ate breakfast in the kitchen before settling down in the computer room, known affectionately around the Farm as "the Bear's Lair."

Over the years, Kurtzman had refined his sophisticated computer network to the point that while he slept, the equipment still effectively monitored the data output of other organizations and filed all incoming information into categories for quick reference in the morning. In some ways, it was not unlike the morning briefing papers that the Central Intelligence Agency assembled for the President every workday, condensing and analyzing world events in a format the chief executive could skim through prior to tackling his first appointment.

While Kurtzman was browsing through the CIA printouts, Hal Brognola entered the room, carrying a cup of steaming coffee.

"Any word on our boys?"

"Not yet," Kurtzman said. "And they're down to their last three hours."

"Plenty of time, knowing them," Brognola said confidently.

"I hope you're right," Kurtzman said. "I wouldn't mind moving my weight-lifting equipment into a nice new gymnasium."

Brognola grinned. "Yeah, and I've always wanted to get a few horses out here. Well, we'll just have to—"

"Hold it," Kurtzman cut in, suddenly racing his fingers across the keyboard of his main computer.

"What do you have?"

"This is the Secret Service file," Kurtzman said, indicating the material being flashed across the screen. "Take a look at that hospital report."

"Rabters?" Brognola read. He set down his coffee mug, startled. "In a coma? When the hell did this happen?"

Kurtzman punched a few more keys. "Yesterday morning. Freeway accident. On his way to work after talking to you, I guess...."

"And he's been in a coma all this time?" There was increased alarm in the chief's voice.

"That's what it says." Then it dawned on Kurtzman. "Oh, no, are you thinking what I'm thinking?"

"I sure as hell am!" Brognola lurched across the room and grabbed a wall phone. As he started dialing, he called over his shoulder, "I'm calling the Service. Try to patch through to the Team and tell 'em no one out there knows what's going down!"

THE PREVIOUS NIGHT, Gadgets Schwarz's stint at the computer had proved more than fruitful, and he attained several important bits of information about the President's movements the following morning. Foremost, he learned that due to unexpected hopes of a major breakthrough in his talks with members of the Central America Federation, the President had moved his scheduled nine-thirty breakfast meeting at the Northgate Hotel ahead an hour so that he could reconvene at ten with the CAF cadre. The CAF talks were to be held in the Pan American Union on Seventeenth and Constitution, less than two blocks from the Northgate.

Able Team would make the hit when the President was transferring between buildings. Toward that end, Schwarz's second coup had been in securing blueprint layouts of both buildings along with the Secret Service's contingency plans for alternate entrances and exits for the President in case of emergency. The weakest link seemed to be at the Northgate, where the alternate exit took the President through the complex's kitchen area.

To create the necessary diversions and otherwise set up their quickly formulated plan, Able Team relied on a combination of guile, chutzpah and deception, but by morning things were solidly in place and the men were ready for the big moment. They'd left their communicators behind so that any untimely paging signals wouldn't blow their cover. Thus, Aaron Kurtzman's frantic SOS to them went unheard and unheeded.

It was too late to warn Able Team that any attempt on the President would be treated as genuine.

Thanks to an anonymous phone tip, the anti-CAF demonstrators who had picketed the White House the night before were on hand at the Northgate, placards in hand, shouting their displeasure with the President, who was breakfasting in the private banquet room with senators Vellen and Anderson of the subcommittee on foreign affairs, no doubt testing the waters for possible reactions to new terms in a peace initiative for Central America.

Gadgets, disguised only by horn-rimmed glasses and a loose-fitting muslin pullover to match the Central American garb of many of the demonstrators, had arrived alone with a dozen protest signs nailed to wooden sticks. He had passed out the signs without incident and now blended in with the crowd outside the Northgate's main entrance. Secret Service officers, joined by local police, were watching the crowd to ensure that it didn't get out of hand.

After a few minutes, once Schwarz had established a camaraderie with several protesters, he suggested, "I doubt the President's going to be coming out this way. Maybe some of us should move around to the side."

"Good idea," one of them replied.

The Northgate was situated on a corner, so its side entrance also faced a major street. Therefore, the sidewalks in front of it could legally be used for peaceful demonstration, a fact that one of the anti-CAF organizers pointed out to an overzealous D.C. cop who tried to dissuade them from congregating near the second doorway. There was a further brief discussion of whether local loitering ordinances superseded the constitutional right to free speech and assembly, and when the matter was settled in favor of the demonstrators, the policeman backed off.

Gadgets checked his watch.

9:48.

According to the Secret Service timetable, the President was to leave the Northgate in two minutes. Glancing down the street, Gadgets saw the presidential limousine pull up in front of the Northgate, and the police cordon off the walkway from the front doors to the curb, holding back the jeering demonstrators.

"I'll be damned," the man next to Schwarz said. "Looks like he's going to come through us, after all."

"How about that," Schwarz replied casually, although he knew better. He checked his watch again, then excused himself to go across the street to make a phone call. On the way he counted off the seconds, waiting for the Team's plan to click into high gear.

Suddenly, a series of small, caplike explosions and bursts of smoke arose from the crowd. Schwarz had embedded small, harmless charges into the staffs of the twelve protest signs, each programmed by means of a microchip detonator to go off at precisely 9:59. The effect was dramatic.

Both the demonstrators and law enforcement personnel were taken aback. In the ensuing pandemonium, the presidential limousine screeched away from the curb without its intended passenger. Behind the

Northgate, a second vehicle idled, ready to advance to a designated alternate exit seconds before the President would emerge. Since the mysterious explosions occurred near both street doorways, it was likely that the backup limo would speed down a back alley to the rear service entrance.

"What the hell's going on out there!" cried out Secret Service agent Mike Aanero, who was standing guard inside the Northgate near the closed doors behind which the President was just concluding his meeting with the senators.

"We're not sure," responded a second agent who came rushing back from the lobby. "Something going down at both entrances, though. We're going to have to take him out the back."

The door behind them opened and two more Secret Service agents led the President and the senators into the hallway.

"This way, sir," Aanero told the President, gesturing away from the lobby.

"Why's that?"

"A change in plans, sir," Aanero said. Another officer flanked the President on the other side and they headed down the corridor as the other two agents detained the senators.

"There's something wrong, isn't there?" said Senator Anderson, a tall, rail-thin man, as he glanced toward the lobby.

"Everything's under control," the agent closest to him responded as he unclipped a walkie-talkie that had beeped to life on his belt. He held the receiver to his mouth and snapped, "This is Agent Richard."

The call was being relayed from Beltsville, and Richard's jaw dropped as he received the belated news of the wager between Rabters and Brognola. By the time he signed off and broke away from the senators, the President and his armed escorts were nearing the kitchen.

THE NORTHGATE HOTEL, like any other publicity-conscious establishment, liked to accommodate the press, and when the production staff of a local radio morning show called the previous evening, wondering if the Northgate would be interested in being a last-minute addition to a feature segment on prime dining spots around Capitol Hill, the answer from management had been an unequivocal yes.

The two-man crew, consisting of an interviewer and sound man, had arrived early that morning. Equipped with the necessary credentials, they were cleared by the Secret Service to proceed with their business, and advised to keep away from the banquet facilities where the presidential breakfast would be taking place. The hotel's manager and maître d' had already been interviewed. To wrap up the segment, the production crew had gone into the kitchen to talk to the head chef, Joaquin Colmas, who was proudly describing the breakfast he had just prepared for the President.

"...And the breakfast rolls were made here fresh this morning, of course," the man concluded, glancing self-consciously at the boom microphone being held above him by sound man Pol Blancanales.

"Well, that certainly whets *my* appetite," Carl Lyons said, holding a second microphone. Like Blancanales, he wore the same disguise as the night before. Patting Colmas on the shoulder, he said, "And I have no doubt but that somewhere down the hall, the President's saying 'Hail to the Chef,' right?"

Colmas laughed uneasily. "Yes, that would be very nice."

In fact, at that moment the President was being led through the swinging inside doors of the kitchen by his Secret Service escorts.

"Move aside, please," Agent Aanero called to Colmas, Lyons and Blancanales.

"But of course," Lyons said.

The next few seconds seemed to drag by in slow motion, each beat filled with a charged tension and drama. Lyons and Blancanales broke away from the chef and calmly stepped back to make room for the Presidential entourage. They simultaneously brought their well-camouflaged blowguns into play. In a sweeping motion, Blancanales lowered the three-foot hollow pole supporting his boom mike and, aiming it at the President, put one end to his lips. Lyons did the same with his hand-held microphone, which was likewise hollowed out in the middle.

The President winced as Blancanales's shot struck him in the forehead with a barely discernible slap. A split second later, the second pellet raised a welt on his neck, near the carotid artery. Both stinging blows also left reddish stains.

"Able Team two, Secret Service nothing," Lyons barked into the stunned silence as he lowered his mike.

Agent Aanero had no idea what Lyons was talking about. His well-honed instincts told him an assassination attempt was in progress, and as his partner lunged between the President and his supposed assassins, Aanero jerked out his service revolver. Six feet away, Lyons and Blancanales were close enough to be easy targets. They had no time to duck.

As Aanero pressed his finger on the trigger, however, a hand reached out and grabbed his wrist, throwing off his aim. One slug zinged past Lyons's ear and clanged loudly off a copper pot hanging from a rack behind him.

"It's okay!" the President shouted, shaking off the second agent and retaining his grip on Aanero's gun-hand. "It's okay, damn it!"

Chef Colmas was in a dead faint on the floor. Across the room, other cooks were diving for cover. Then the kitchen doors burst inward again, admitting the Secret Service agent who had received the call from Beltsville.

"Wait, I just got word that Able Team..." His voice trailed off as he took in the bizarre tableau that confronted him.

For the second time in less than two minutes, Agent Aanero exclaimed, "What the hell's going on?"

Lyons stepped forward and yanked the revolver from Aanero's hand. Even through his makeup, the

Ironman's face was flushed with rage at nearly taking a bullet to the brain. "That's what I'd like to know!"

Releasing Aanero, the President eyed Lyons and Blancanales, and rubbed his "wounds." He muttered, "I'm sure as hell glad you guys are on my side."

8

Before leaving Central America, Sergei Karanov had called his most trusted contacts within America's so-called Bible Belt, people who owed him favors and could be counted on to be discreet about their involvement with him. Three of them, part-time Soviet contract agents, had recently put Karanov up in San Diego after his flight from the KGB, and helped him put together the nest egg he'd been living off in Rio for the past months. Two of the three, the volatile father-and-son team of Lee B. and Dale James, were in Tennessee, spying on nuclear research facilities in the high-tech corridor between Knoxville and Oak Ridge, and at Karanov's request had agreed to drive to Nashville and put Roxanne and Brian Darling under surveillance. The others were bound for downstate Memphis, where Karanov had scheduled a rendezvous the following night.

Sergei Karanov arrived in Memphis by way of Miami, exhausted by the long flight from San Leon City. He took a cab to the King Hotel on Elvis Presley Boulevard, and checked in under the pseudonym Texas John Richniel. It was only two in the afternoon, so leaving instructions at the desk for a wake-up call at six, he collapsed in bed, falling asleep in his clothes.

Five hours, a shower and a meal later, Karanov was dressed down in Levi's and a corduroy jacket and heading north by cab toward the skyscrapers of downtown Memphis. Even though Graceland was closed for the night, a throng of die-hard Elvis fans maintained a vigil outside the famed gates, staring devoutly at the rock-and-roll legend's mansion on the hill.

"Folks sure do love Elvis, don't they?" Karanov remarked, trying out his accent on the cabbie.

"Named the damn road after him, fer God's sake, I should hope they love him," the man behind the wheel retorted, talking around a toothpick that bobbed between his teeth. "Me, I'll take Chuck Berry every time. Sumbitch is sixty fucking years old and still lean and mean. Wrote his own shit, too."

"Ain't that the truth," Karanov conceded. He and the driver talked music all the way into town. By then the sun was a memory and the city gleamed with its own light. Karanov walked down to Beale Street, where the nightlife was just getting under way.

In efforts to make the reputed birthplace of the blues more of a tourist mecca, most of Beale Street had been closed off to traffic, and major renovations were in progress at numerous addresses. Stretching eastward from posh condominiums overlooking the Mississippi, the revitalized strip boasted more than thirty restaurants, nightclubs, shops and boutiques as well as several parks where pickup musicians played for tips, competing with the live jazz and blues featured in the indoor showcases. Horse-drawn carriages hauled couples around the sights and policemen on bicycles assured the many pedestrians that law and order was close at hand.

Karanov bought a flavored wine cooler from a sidewalk vendor in front of the New Daisy Theater, then strolled to the end of the block, where a crowd was gathered in a small park, listening to a hunchbacked bluesman sing an old Jelly Roll Morton song on the front porch of the small house where W.C. Handy, father of the blues, was born. The Russian listened admiringly to the old man's stunning guitar work and self-accompaniment on the harmonica. He was doubly impressed when the song ended and he found out the man, who wore tinted glasses, was blind.

Over the next twenty minutes, while the blind man played a handful of blues standards, Karanov was joined one by one by his trusted associates. There were six in all, and the last to arrive was Dennis Gent, who told the group he'd rented a room at the nearby Banner Hotel. Agreeing that they would feel freer to speak in private, after the blind man's set they dispersed with the rest of the crowd, and walked in pairs so as not to arrive at the Banner all at once.

Karanov walked with Dale James, a twenty-year-old physics whiz and the son of Lee B. James, who was still in Nashville watching the Darlings. Karanov had met Dale during an assignment in Knoxville six years ago, and had persuaded the youth and his father to help steal secrets from a nuclear research facility where Dale worked summers as a bicycle courier. At fourteen, the James boy was a chip off his father's block, and in the years since he had only furthered his reputation while attending the University of Tennessee.

"We had no trouble tracking down either of them," Dale told Karanov as they walked up Third Street. "Roxanne spent all day at the recording studio, working on a new album. She's supposed to be meeting some old friend at her house tomorrow morning, I heard."

"You checked out security?" Karanov asked.

Dale nodded. "There's a lot of people going in and out of the studio, and security's pretty tight. Her house seems a better bet. She's got a private guard and a couple dogs, but other than that just a fence and the usual alarm system."

"What about her brother?"

Dale laughed. "He's no problem. Has a dinky little apartment near Centennial Park, a cinch to get into. He seems to be out of it."

"How do you mean?"

"Depressed, absentminded." The youth boasted, "I could have offed him a few times just today."

"I appreciate your restraint," Karanov told him. "We want him alive until we can get them both together."

"You gonna let us in on what this is all about?" Dale asked.

"I'll let you know what you need to know. Trust me, it's in your interest not to know the whole picture."

Dale nodded. "That's cool."

"I knew you would understand," the Russian said, patting the younger man on the back paternally. "Tell me, how are you and the old man getting along these days?"

"Hah!" Dale spit into the street. "Same old shit as always. He thinks he's got me on a fucking leash and wigs out when I do anything on my own. Man, he's so nickel-and-dime...never going to get anywhere in this life and he wants to drag me down with him. Pisses me off."

"He tries his best," Karanov offered diplomatically. "You have to give him that."

"Yeah, well his best ain't much." Dale looked at Karanov with unabashed admiration, as a disciple would his mentor. "You showed me more of the ropes in a few months than he has in twenty years."

"You're exaggerating a little, don't you think?"

"No way," James insisted. "Look, maybe once we pull this job, you and I can link up. Blow this pop stand and take on the big time. I wanna see the fucking world, damn it!"

"We'll see," Karanov said, secretly pleased by the young man's devotion. Such loyalty could prove handy.

DURING THE MEETING at the Banner, Karanov had the first inkling of a problem he'd hoped to avoid. Jimmy

Lou Bowline, a slick-dressed man in his early fifties who'd driven nonstop to Memphis from the Carolina coast, was normally loud and outspoken, always overeager to dominate any conversation. But now he sat quietly, listening to Karanov lay out the scenario for their mission in Nashville. Whenever Karanov looked his way, Bowline glanced away, cleaning his nails or brushing lint off his suit.

Karanov believed he had survived in the treacherous world of espionage in part because of his ability to read people. He was positive that Jimmy Lou Bowline's atypical behavior was attributable to more than fatigue brought on by his long drive.

Keeping his suspicions to himself, Karanov continued to outline his plan and objectives, making it clear that the shots were being called by Juan Guandaro back in San Leon. Karanov figured that, given the egos of the men he was dealing with, it was better to bring himself as close to their level as possible rather than overemphasize the role of ringleader. The way he laid it out, he was just part of the team, more a quarterback than a coach. Obviously, there were innumerable details that would have to wait until the men were in Nashville, so Karanov outlined a fairly simple strategy. He was finished in fifteen minutes.

Fernando Carlenmach, a prematurely balding man in his twenties with a permanent look of smug condescension, uncrossed his arms and cracked his knuckles. "I know we all owe you, Karanov," he said in a strident, almost petulant voice, "but still, this is asking a lot. I think maybe we could use some more incentive.''

"Man's got a point there,'' another of the men murmured.

Karanov, having anticipated such a situation, wasn't put off by the collective greed in the eyes that faced him.

"Twelve thousand for each man once it's all over,'' he said matter-of-factly, pulling a large envelope from his back pocket. "And two thousand up front. Cash.''

"Hey, now you're talking!'' Dale James exclaimed, clapping his hands.

"Any other questions?'' Karanov asked as he started passing out pre-packaged bundles of fifty-dollar bills to each man, starting with Bowline. "Jimmy Lou?''

Bowline hesitated a moment, then lapsed into his normal self for the first time all evening, sniffing the money as if it were fresh-baked bread. "Mmm, I just want to know the way to Lansky's. Got to buy me some new threads!''

"No shit,'' Carlenmach taunted. "You look like a goddamn Charleston pimp, Jimmy Lou!''

"That so?'' Bowline shot back. "You want, I'll take you out back and leave you lookin' like New Orleans gumbo.''

"Ooh, hot air from the coast.''

"All right, that's enough,'' Karanov said. "Let's leave in pairs the same way we came in. We'll meet to-morrow morning in Nashville.''

"Well, I'm headin' back to Beale Street," Carlenmach said, giving Bowline a nudge. "How about you, Jimmy Lou? What say we bury the hatchet and tie one on, eh?"

"No can do," Bowline said. "I gotta do some dozin', know what I mean? I been on the road so long I'm still seein' white lines."

"Speakin' of white lines," said Chuck Scott, another of the conspirators, "I'm gonna score me some toot with this chump change."

As the men started to file out, Karanov took Dennis Gent and Dale James aside and whispered, "I'm going to need you to help me take care of something before we leave town...."

UPON LEAVING the elevator, Jimmy Lou Bowline broke away on the excuse that he had to make a phone call, ducked into a booth in the front lobby and flipped through the yellow pages until the other conspirators had left the hotel. Then he nodded through the glass of the phone booth to a stringy-haired, sideburned man with a boxer's flattened nose, who was reading a newspaper in one of the lobby's plush armchairs. Fewer than a dozen people were scattered about the stylish, open-aired area, most of them near the reservation desk.

Glancing at his watch for the benefit of anyone who might be watching, the flat-nosed man stood up and began pacing near the row of public phones as if waiting for a call. When one of the phones rang, he quickly closed himself inside the booth and picked up the receiver.

"He should be down any second," Bowline reported from the phone two booths away. "You got all the exits covered?"

"Of course. What are his plans?"

"Taking care of some business for a friend in Central America," Bowline said. "Some sort of revenge thing up in Nashville. He wants to take out a couple of—"

The door to the Carolinian's booth opened suddenly, and Bowline fell silent as he felt the barrel of a gun burrowing into his ribs. Glancing over his shoulder, he saw Dale James leaning into the booth, holding a Detonics .45 pistol.

"Hang it up, Jimmy Lou . . . nice and easy."

Following orders, Bowline stepped warily out of the booth, seeing that Dennis Gent had similarly put the draw on the man with the broken nose. Gent and James discreetly prodded their captives away from the phones and through a doorway leading to the stairwell.

"Down to the basement," Gent ordered, giving his man a shove.

"What gives, fellas?" Bowline wondered innocently. "Y'all gone loco?"

"Shut up, Jimmy Lou," James warned. "Save your talking for Karanov."

The Banner was undergoing its first major refurbishing in thirty-one years, and the underground parking lot had been temporarily closed and used to store building materials and equipment needed in the multimillion-dollar facelift. Karanov, holding a silenced Beretta, was behind a parked forklift, leaning against a stack of lumber. When James and Gent appeared with their prisoners, the Russian approached the man with the mashed nose. Gent turned over his prisoner to Karanov and studied the forklift, intending to hot-wire the engine.

"Let me guess..." Karanov said, looking closely at the man, then reaching out and jerking off both the wig of stringy hair and the heavy sideburns. "Ah, Uri! So it *is* you! Let's have the nose, too, shall we?"

"Bastard!" Uri cursed over the coughing sputter of the forklift.

"So I am," Karanov said as he peeled the layer of flesh-toned putty from the man's nose, revealing Uri to be a thin-nosed, crew-cut blond in his early forties. Karanov had worked with Uri years before as part of the KGB's dreaded Directorate B, killing renegade agents and other functionaries who had failed in their missions. He knew that the man's presence in Memphis could mean only one thing—that Karanov had been betrayed by Bowline and was marked for execution.

"I don't know what's goin' on here," Jimmy Lou Bowline professed, "but I—"

"Quiet, Jimmy Lou, or you'll die right here," Karanov barked. He turned to Uri and asked, "How many others are here?"

"You'll find out soon enough," Uri sneered.

"Jimmy Lou, maybe you could tell me?"

"Like I said, I don't know nothin' about any of this. I swear!"

Karanov sighed and gestured for Dale James to help him force the two prisoners up against the stack of lumber, so that they were standing side by side, facing the forklift. Behind the controls of the vehicle, Gent slowly raised the twin metal prongs a few feet, then inched the machine forward. Both Uri and Jimmy Lou realized that if the forklift plowed into them, they would be impaled in the vicinity of their manhood.

"I know there's someone across the street from the front entrance," Karanov said, helping the captives out. "Who else?"

"You ran out on the party," Uri calmly told Karanov. "Nothing you do to us will keep you from being liquidated."

"I think you are mistaken," Karanov said. "Gent?"

Gent eased the forklift a few inches closer, so that both Bowline and Uri felt the sharp-edged metal begin to dig into their groins. Uri closed his eyes and gritted his teeth in anticipation of the agony to come. Bowline panicked.

"There's two others!" he blurted desperately. "Mikhail's in the side hallway, and Rodolfo is in a car down the block."

"That's all?" Karanov asked as he motioned for Gent to still the forklift. "No one else is in this?"

"Silence, coward!" Uri hissed at Jimmy Lou.

"No one else!" Bowline insisted, looking away from Uri. "Only those two, Karanov."

"What about the men working with me?" Karanov asked. "What is planned for them?"

"Nothing," Bowline said. "They only want you."

"You're sure, Jimmy Lou?"

"On my mother's grave," the Carolinian vowed.

"Good." Karanov snapped his fingers and Gent put the forklift into reverse, pulling away from the captives. Uri and Bowline relaxed visibly once the pressure was off. Their relief was short-lived. Raising his Beretta, Karanov pumped a spray of 9 mm parabellum into them. The lumber behind them was quickly stained with blood and viscera. The men fell. Bowline's head slammed hard against the concrete floor while Uri's shoulder took the brunt of his fall. Once they hit the ground, neither moved.

"Give me Uri's coat," Karanov ordered James as he placed the dead man's wig atop his bald head, then pressed the fake sideburns into place on his face. "I should be able to slip out easily enough."

"What about our plan?" James asked as he handed over the bloodstained coat. "Are you going to cancel it?"

Karanov shook his head. "No. I've been looking forward to it too much. Besides, it will be my ticket to freedom from the other Uris and Jimmy Lou Bowlines of the world."

9

Saturday lasted forever for Jack Grimaldi. He killed a few hours on Opryland's *General Jackson* steamboat, sampling a stretch of the Cumberland River just east of the city. Among the passengers were fifty Miss America contestants, which reminded Jack that Roxanne Darling had been a finalist as Miss Tennessee a few years before he met her. He wondered how they might have gotten along at that age, and his open laughter at the prospect of a pampered WASP beauty dating a foulmouthed Italian plane jockey drew a few stares. He had a feeling it wouldn't have worked.

From Opryland, he drove southwest to Smyrna, a small town near the massive Percy Pierce Reservoir. During World War II, the town's airfield had been appropriated by the war effort, and fighter pilots had stayed in barracks behind the main terminal before taking to the air in Convair B-24s. Now the Smyrna Air Center was privately owned, although a portion of the facilities were still used by the Air National Guard. Grimaldi had discovered the place on an earlier trip, when he'd befriended the base commandant Milt Neiton over beers at Bill's Landing, a fly-boy bar near the main hangars filled with Air Force memorabilia and frequented by off-duty guardsmen and local workers. Grimaldi met Neiton again that afternoon, and attained permission to take up one of the guard's Iroquois choppers for an aerial tour of the region. Afterward, they reconvened at the Landing for a few hours of drink, conversation and eight ball at one of the bar's two pool tables. It proved an adequate diversion, and by the time Grimaldi returned to his room at the Clarion Maxwell House, it was past eleven.

Still wide awake, Jack turned on the television, but found nothing to his liking. He was about to flick off the set when he came across a news broadcast. He remembered Able Team's wager and watched for news of an attempt on the President, knowing that the twenty-four-hour deadline had passed. The lead story concerned a gangland-style execution that had occurred only an hour before in the basement of Memphis's Banner Hotel. Grimaldi was intrigued by the few details the reporter was able to divulge. The killing had all the makings of a Mafia hit, and he wondered if the syndicate might be on the verge of the shake-up that had been anticipated since the imprisonment of several Midwestern dons whom Able Team had helped to keep behind bars the previous spring.

Once the newscast had degenerated into filler stories about charity raffles and the latest wrinkles in contract negotiations between the Nashville Sounds minor league franchise and its major league affiliate, Grimaldi gave in to his curiosity and called Stony Man

Farm, taking the usual circuitous phone route to assure a clean line.

"Hey, Bear," Jack said when he recognized Kurtzman's voice on the line. "It's Grimaldi. I didn't get you out of bed, did I?"

"No, Jack. You know I'm a night owl. Nashville treating you all right?"

"Just fine, Bear. Look, I just want to know how the guys fared in D.C."

"Well . . ." Kurtzman taunted Grimaldi with a prolonged pause, then divulged, "We're getting ourselves a new gym!"

"All right!" Jack exclaimed. "How'd it go down?"

Kurtzman briefly explained the nearly fatal snafu that had almost ruined Able Team's victory, concluding, "I think this was the first time that the President saved a Secret Service agent instead of the other way around. Lyons was ready to kill the guy who almost shot him."

"Can you blame him?" Jack said. "Hell, I'd love to have been there. How'd they manage to keep it out of the press?"

"All they had to do was get the chef and his cooks to swear to silence," Kurtzman explained. "There were a few media people around curious about the protesters' exploding signs, but since Gadgets had changed by then and nobody could put a finger on him, the whole thing was dismissed as a publicity ploy by the demonstrators."

"So the guys are okay?" Grimaldi asked.

"Yeah. Last I heard they were indulging in some seven-course meal at a posh restaurant in Georgetown. President's picking up the tab," Kurtzman said. "We're giving 'em a few days off after that."

Hearing a knock at his door, Grimaldi bade Kurtzman a quick farewell. "Who is it?" he called out.

"Brian Darling," came a voice out of Jack's past.

WHEN I LAST SAW you, you were a zit-faced know-it-all driving your sister's band around in the old man's station wagon," Grimaldi told Brian in an isolated booth at an all-night family restaurant across from Maxwell House.

"Well, my acne's cleared up and I own my own car now," Brian said, blushing slightly. "Roxanne needs a couple semis to get around when she tours these days."

"Times change, don't they?"

A uniformed waitress took their orders. Both men wanted only coffee.

"Sis mentioned you were in town," Brian said after the waitress filled their cups and left. "I know I'm probably out of line butting in before you've even had a chance to see her, but . . ."

"No problem," Jack said. "All you took me away from was 'Saturday Night Live.' No big loss there."

"That's good."

"Something wrong, Brian?" Grimaldi asked, noticing his uneasiness. "You seem a little on edge."

Brian nodded. He wasn't sure where to begin, and after adding a container of nondairy creamer to his coffee, blurted out, "Did you kill anybody when you were in Nam?"

Grimaldi tried to keep a straight face. Not that he was particularly proud of it, but he'd killed a lot of men, in Nam and in all the years since then. Something told him this wasn't a statistic Brian needed to know, so he answered, "Most people who went over there had some death on their hands by the time they came back. Why?"

"How'd you feel about it?"

"Depended on the circumstances," Grimaldi admitted. "Usually I felt lousy. Other times...well, you saw a buddy get blown away one second and the next second you got a chance to nail the bastard who did it, that was another matter."

"Was it harder when you saw the face of someone you killed?"

Jack took a long sip of coffee, and looked around to make sure no one was in earshot. Then he leaned forward, looked Darling in the eyes and quietly asked, "Who did you kill, Brian?"

Brian recoiled visibly, as if hearing the words aloud added a whole new dimension of terror to his private torment. He whispered hoarsely, "I'm not really sure that I killed them."

"Them?"

His trembling hands were generating waves in his coffee cup. "Maybe this wasn't a good idea," he mumbled.

"Come on, Brian. Talk to me, all right?"

Talk Brian did. For the better part of thirty minutes, he spilled out the details of his involvement with the Crusade for Conscience and the aborted rendezvous in San Leon City that had led to his taking a gun into his hands for the first time and using it to escape from the courtyard on Avenida Missione. Jack listened impassively, unable to reveal that he knew all about the atrocities of El Chocomil del Sangre from reports by Stony Man Farm's own connections in Central America. Although he sensed the meager efforts of the CFC were futile in comparison with more direct intervention from a group like Able Team or Phoenix Force, Grimaldi couldn't help but admire the dogged determination of those who attempted to change the world with the seemingly antiquated notion that the pen was mightier than the sword.

When Brian had ended his revelations, Grimaldi asked, "How much of this does your sister know?"

"Not much," Darling conceded miserably. "She knows I'm involved...or at least that I was involved with CFC, but I couldn't bring myself to tell her that I went on the USO tour mainly to make the rendezvous with Keliersa and Herton."

"Why not?"

Brian fiddled with his now-empty coffee cup. "At first, I didn't want her to talk me out of going. And after...after, I was too ashamed."

The waitress came by offering refills, but Grimaldi put a hand over his cup and asked for the check. When they were alone again, he told Brian, "You don't have anything to be ashamed of. You tried to do things idealistically, and when the shit hit the fan you fell back on your instincts and did what the situation called for. You want my opinion, you did the right thing."

"But I'm supposed to believe in nonviolence."

"Good, then still believe in it. But Brian, this isn't the best of all possible worlds, and there's times when we just can't ignore that fact. Have you stopped to think what might have happened if you hadn't grabbed that gun? You'd either be dead or missing out in the hills of San Leon somewhere with some thugs trimming your eyelids with a razor trying to convince you to talk. How do you think your sister would have felt then?"

Brian shuddered at this description of torture and felt renewed shame at having misled Roxanne. He was relieved to have talked out his dilemma with Grimaldi, but he was still confused, lost in the quagmire of his conflicting emotions.

"What do you think I should do?" he asked the older man.

"For starters, I think you should get your ass back into CFC and keep on trying to make things work the way they should. I got a feeling they need all the good people they can get, and from the sounds of it you're probably one of the aces up their sleeve.

"And secondly, I think you owe your sister an explanation. Hell, wiped out as you look, she's probably thinking you're dying of cancer or the clap, for Christ's sake!"

Brian forced a grin and reached for the bill when the waitress delivered it. Grimaldi beat him to it.

"Come on," Brian said, "I'm the one who dragged you over here...."

"Nobody drags me anywhere I don't want to go," he said, putting a few dollars on the table and rising. He walked with Brian to the exit. "Tell you what, you want to do me a favor, let me in on your sister's love life the past few years. How many hearts has she broken since mine?"

"I think you should probably ask her that yourself," Brian said as they stepped into the humid night. "You're going to be seeing her in the morning, aren't you? I can tell you she's looking forward to it."

"In that case, you bet your ass I'll be there," Jack wisecracked.

"You thinking of staying in town awhile?" Brian asked. "You know, trying to get something serious going between you two?"

"Whoa, whoa!" Jack said. "One thing at a time. We haven't even talked in thirteen years. Who's to say we'll even hit it off these days?"

"Look at you and me," Brian said. "Listen, I really want to thank you for listening to me back in there."

"Glad if it helped," Grimaldi said.

"It did. Thanks again, Jack."

Grimaldi watched the younger man drive off. Once traffic cleared, he jogged across the street to his hotel. It was past midnight now. Only a few hours until he saw Roxanne. He hoped he'd be able to get to sleep.

10

After dinner in Georgetown, Able Team repaired to Keith's Korner, a tavern down the block that turned out to be a favorite watering hole for university students. The carefree, boisterous atmosphere of the bar contrasted sharply with the subdued mood of the three men. Carl Lyons, in particular, had been feeling troubled since dinner, and the sight of so many young, ebullient faces soon became more than he could handle.

"This is getting to be pretty depressing," he said as he poured the last of his Heineken into a frosted mug. "Let's slide these brews down the hatch and hit it."

"Hey, we just got here," Blancanales said. "Relax and enjoy yourself."

"Look at them, willya?" Lyons groaned. "Green behind the ears but they still think they have all the answers. Makes me feel old, damn it. I should have ordered Geritol."

Pol and Gadgets looked at each other and laughed.

"Nothing like a bullet by the ear to make a guy think about his mortality, eh?" Schwarz razzed, giving Lyons a nudge.

"Poke me again, Schwarz, and you'll be doing one-handed pushups because the other one'll be missing!"

"Hey, easy, friend," Gadgets said. "We're here for a nightcap, remember? The idea's to relax."

"Yeah, amigo," Blancanales piped in. "Or at least to gloat a little. This was a big day for us, *si*? Played tag with the President and won ourselves a gymnasium, had a hundred-dollar dinner of the best damn cow this side of the Rockies. Shit, we should be whooping it up like those guys in the beer commercials. How about it, big guy?"

Lyons stared down his Heineken, then drained it in one long swallow before rising from his table. "Sorry, guys, but I'm just out of it tonight. I think I'll get back to the hotel and turn in. Maybe I'll wake up in a better mood."

"Suit yourself," Blancanales told him.

Schwarz said, "You want some company?"

Lyons shook his head and elbowed his way through the sea of off-duty law students until he was out of the bar. The street was crawling with taxis, and he had no trouble flagging one down. As it inched through the logjam of traffic, the driver, who was in his twenties, asked Lyons, "Hey, don't you teach poli sci in East Hall?"

"No."

"You're not faculty?"

"Sorry."

"Huh. I could swear I've seen you on campus."

"You must be thinking of someone else," Lyons said. "I teach at the school of hard knocks."

The cabbie laughed and patted the dashboard. "I take a few classes there, too."

"Look, nothing personal, but I've got a few things on my mind, okay?"

"Sorry," the driver apologized, turning his attention back to his driving. The traffic flow thinned out once they cleared Georgetown and passed over Rock Creek. To his right, Lyons could see the well-illuminated presidential monuments, but the scenery barely registered in his mind. He was too busy trying to get a handle on his frayed nerves, to figure out what was bothering him.

He knew it had something to do with this town and the heady essence of politics that seemed to exude from its very pores. All through dinner, he'd watched the town's power brokers peddling their influence at the other tables, making deals over filet mignon and exotic side dishes with names he couldn't even pronounce. And everyone, men and women alike, wore the same indulgent, self-satisfied smile, as if their enjoyment of the perquisites of their positions was infinitely more important than their actual usefulness to the people they were supposed to serve. He hadn't enjoyed his meal, and later, when Able Team had moved to the bar, it seemed as if this younger generation were drooling to pursue the same self-serving dreams of their Capitol Hill predecessors. Just what this country needed was more overpaid lawyers and political blowhards, Lyons thought to himself cynically.

Or, he wondered, was he just another discontented have-not bitching because he hadn't yet had a chance to feed at the trough of opulence? It hardly seemed the case. Hell, Able Team's countless escapades over the years had provided ample opportunity to siphon off the loot of vanquished foes or cut deals with the powers-that-be for enough money to support a lifestyle that would turn even the most jaded Washingtonian green with envy. But he and Schwarz and Blancanales always resisted such temptations, contenting themselves with smaller rewards, like an indoor gymnasium or a chance to break in some new piece of weaponry fresh from the workbench of Stony Man's ace armorer, Cowboy Kissinger.

"Or maybe I'm just getting to be a crank in my old age," Lyons muttered to himself.

"What was that?" the driver said.

"Nothing."

By now they were in Maryland, driving past the green expanse of Anacostia Park. In another five minutes they reached the Attaché. Lyons tipped the driver heavily, then trudged inside and took the elevator to the thirteenth floor. As he was unlocking the door of Able Team's suite, he heard a noise behind him and, turning, saw three armed men in suits pour out of the room across the hall.

"Freeze!" one of them cried out.

If they were hoping for an easy surrender, they'd picked the wrong man at the wrong time. With a banshee cry, Lyons unleashed his pent-up emotions with a limb-flailing display of Shotokan karate. The gunman closest to him crumpled to the floor, the wind knocked from his lungs, and a second man took a blow to the side of the head that sent him reeling. Unfortunately, Lyons was unable to reach the final attacker before the butt of an automatic pistol clipped him behind the right ear. Staggering, he knocked over a potted rubber plant, fighting to remain conscious. It was a losing battle. Within seconds, he succumbed to the creeping void.

WHEN HE CAME TO, Lyons found himself propped up in a chair inside Able Team's penthouse suite with his wrists and ankles handcuffed. His skull throbbed with pain, as if a demolition derby was taking place between his ears.

"Ah, Mr. Backles, you've rejoined us at last!"

Through the asteroid shower obscuring Lyons's vision he discerned the figure of a man in a suit pacing before him. Tall and gaunt, with small patches of reddish hair around his huge pointed ears, he reminded Lyons of a Vulcan on "Star Trek."

"Mr. Backles, are you with us?"

"Backles?" Lyons groaned.

"That's what it says here," the suited man said, holding out a laminated press card with a photo of Lyons in his dark hair and mustache disguise. "But then, that must be a nom de plume, since you really don't work for the *Guardian* and you've obviously changed back to your natural look."

"Yeah, I decided blondes do have more fun," Lyons told his interrogator. "Mind telling me who the fuck you are?"

The man in the suit clucked his tongue. "Now, now, such language. How about if you let me ask the questions?"

Turning, Lyons saw the two others who had accosted him. One had an ice pack pressed against his face, while the other held his sore ribs and smoked a cigarette. The memory of having leveled them made Lyons grin. "Two out of three ain't bad," he thought.

"We've already looked around here," the man on his feet explained, gesturing to the opened suitcases on the far bed, which had been filled with the paraphernalia Able Team had used in plotting its hit on the President. "Why don't you help us get to bed at a decent hour and tell us who's backing you?"

"Mattel," Lyons drawled. "We're toy salesmen. Wanna buy a few things for the kids? Christmas isn't that far off, you know."

"Don't make this hard on us or you'll regret it." The man with Vulcan ears squatted on his haunches so that he stared directly into Lyons's face. "We know you're linked up with the anti-CAF people who've been demonstrating here all weekend. Last night our undercover men photographed you in front of the White House, so don't bother denying it. We just want to know who's bankrolling you."

Despite his pain, Lyons tilted his head back and roared with laughter.

"Something funny?"

Lyons nodded, bringing himself under control. "You guys are Bureau, right?"

"That's correct."

"Don't you guys bother to compare notes with the Secret Service?"

The pointed-ears man frowned uncertainly. "What's that supposed to mean?"

Lyons snickered again. When the door to the suite swung inward and he saw more plainclothes officers leading in Blancanales and Schwarz, who were also handcuffed, he nearly fell out of his chair laughing.

"Gee, guys, looks like dey put da collar on yous, too," Lyons said, talking with a Brooklyn accent. "I guess da gig's up, huh, boss?"

"Yeah, that's right, Rocko," Schwarz countered with an Edward G. Robinson impersonation. "Looks like the G-men got us nailed dead to rights."

"We're goin' down the river?" Blancanales played along, dropping to his knees with mock horror. He pleaded to the pointed-ears man, "*Madre de Dios,* I'm only a boy! Please have mercy!"

The bureau agent raised his voice in anger, warning, "You're just digging your graves deeper."

"Correction, pal," Lyons said, dropping the shtick. "You're the ones setting yourselves up for the big fall."

"Meaning what?" Pointed Ears demanded.

"Why don't you pick up the phone and dial Beltsville?" Lyons suggested. "Ask the Service about the President's blowgun party this morning and tell 'em you're sitting on the guys who did it. See what kind of medals this is gonna get you."

The Bureau head signaled for one of his underlings to make the call. In less than two minutes, Able Team was duly identified and the collective embarrassment on the part of the FBI men threatened to choke everyone in the room.

"We could still nail your ass for resisting arrest," Pointed Ears threatened Lyons, as he removed his handcuffs.

"And we could see to it that you and your merry men are the laughingstock of the Bureau," Lyons countered. "You decide."

It took only a few seconds for the feds to realize that a strategic retreat was in order. Without so much as apologizing for the false arrest and detainment, the suited men filed out of the room, leaving Able Team behind. Lyons retrieved the ice pack from the bed and put it against his head.

"Damn, Ironman," Pol wisecracked, "if we'd known you were ducking out on us for this, we would have come along. Shoot, all we got was a little strongarm treatment in the elevators."

"Can it," Lyons said, slamming the lid on his suitcase. "I've had it with this town."

11

In a gesture meant to draw community attention to its efforts, the Crusade for Conscience held its monthly Sunday meeting in front of the Metropolitan Courthouse, an imposing fifty-year-old monolith that housed the city government. The building was one of the most ornate and expensive in downtown Nashville, and its outer doors boasted bronze sculptures representing individual human traits thought to be American ideals. For their meeting, CFC officials had chosen to gather outside the door representing Justice.

"...And Justice is what our organization stands for and works for," Frank Hirsh explained, directing his introductory remarks to the small press contingent and a handful of prospective new members mingling among the two dozen card-carrying followers. "Primarily, we are involved in letter-writing campaigns on behalf of individuals known to be either falsely imprisoned or else behind bars solely for the nonviolent expression of their political beliefs. In addition, we work in coordination with our national office in undertaking fact-finding missions abroad where there have been extensive reports of human rights violations.

"On that front, we've been concentrating our efforts lately on Central America, which, as you know, has become increasingly volatile in recent months, despite the U.N.'s presence.

"In fact, I'd like to start out the meeting by updating the situation down there. Just last week one of our former members was down in San Leon City trying to get some information on—"

"A *current* member was down there," Brian Darling called out as he pushed through the throng and climbed the steps to where Hirsh was speaking. The men traded glances, and Brian offered a telling half grin.

"Welcome back to the fold," Hirsh said privately to Brian, before stepping away from the portable podium.

Taking Hirsh's place, Brian proceeded to detail his visit to the troubled country and his involvement in the ambush on Avenida Missione, though he deliberately avoided mention of any shooting. Although the snapping of cameras was disconcerting, he'd decided to honor his commitment to the Crusade, and accepted the fact that media coverage was a valuable tool in spreading word of its efforts. He spoke not only with conviction but with passion as well, concluding, "The fact that El Chocomil resorted to such drastic measures against us is a good indication of just how vital our mission is, and what a difference it can make. The secret police of San Leon would like nothing better than to intimidate the outside world from shedding light on their affairs, and that's all the more reason for you to back the CFC any way you can. Write to your elected officials and demand that they act to end the reign of terror in San Leon. Here in Nashville, Congressman Will has steadfastly refused to do anything on this issue, and it's up to us to continue pressuring him until he attempts to make those in power in Washington take their heads out of the sand. It's vital that we push and push and continue to push until the Crusade for Conscience becomes obsolete because the world has finally opened its eyes and decided to put an end to false imprisonment and human rights violations.''

There was an unexpected wave of applause, and Brian blushed as he moved away from the podium. Hirsh, standing beside him, whispered, ''Quite a change of heart since I last talked to you. What happened?''

''I just got a little encouragement from an old acquaintance,'' Brian said, referring to Jack Grimaldi.

''Well, you sure as hell passed the encouragement along, Bri. Good work.''

Hirsh took over the podium and began a review of the CFC's present slate of letter-writing campaigns and fact-finding operations. Brian headed back into the crowd and sat down, acknowledging further congratulations from longtime members. Two reporters came over to him requesting interviews. He told them he'd be happy to oblige them another time, but he had other commitments. No sooner had they moved away than a young man in a suit sat down next to Brian and extended his hand.

"Hi, Mr. Darling, my name's Mark Douglas."

"Hello, Mark. Call me Brian, okay?"

"Sure. Brian, I came here specifically in hopes of seeing you. I have friends in San Leon that work with the Catholic church's radio. The station broadcasts nationwide there and is exempted from censorship, so they can report the news impartially and—"

"Yes," Brian interrupted, "I'm familiar with the station."

"Then you know that they also play a lot of inspirational songs, some with specific messages of hope for our people." When Brian nodded, the man in the suit continued, "Well, after your sister's appearance at the U.N. troop base, my friends came up with the idea of asking her if she might record a song or two on behalf of the human rights movement down there."

"It's a good idea, but I'm afraid I can't speak for my sister," Brian said.

"But you could speak *to* her, couldn't you?" Douglas pressed. "She is a favorite singer in San Leon, you know. The Spanish versions she does of some of her songs are played all the time."

"I know, but she has so many commitments and demands on her time...."

"My people would be willing to pay for the recording session. And here, I have the song with me." He handed Brian a lyric sheet with a San Leon post-office-box address stamped in the upper corner.

"This song is by David Keliersa!" Brian exclaimed, seeing the dead folksinger's name at the top of the sheet.

"Yes," the other man said. "We found it among his personal effects. As you can imagine, it might prove to be a real inspiration to our people if it were to be released, especially with your sister singing."

"It would," Brian conceded, still staring at the sheet, "but—"

"All I ask is that you give this to her and let her decide. It would be a vital service for our cause...and yours, too, of course. Not to mention being a fitting last tribute to David."

Nodding, Brian folded the sheet and put it in his pocket. "I'll see what I can do."

"Thanks so much," Douglas said. "Do you have any idea when you'll be seeing Roxanne? We're anxious to start on this as soon as possible, or at least to find another singer to record it if she isn't available."

Brian looked at his watch. "As a matter of fact, I'm heading out to her place for brunch in a few minutes. I can let her know about this immediately."

"Wonderful," Douglas said, rising. "You can reach me at the number at the bottom of the sheet." He shook Brian's hand again. "Thanks again, so much."

Douglas retreated to the back of the crowd, where he leaned against a concrete waste receptacle. He half listened to the meeting in progress, but kept his eyes on Brian. When Darling rose toward the end of the meeting and headed down the steps to his parked Nova, the man in the suit took a small digital clock from his pocket, and set it ten minutes later than the actual time. With equal nonchalance, he opened a paper bag from a nearby fast food establishment. Inside was a compact bomb consisting primarily of powerful C-4 plastic explosives. A clock affixed to the detonating device showed the correct time. The man linked it with the second clock, thereby beginning a deadly countdown.

Dropping the bag into the concrete container, Douglas left the gathering, taking long strides down Charlotte Avenue until he reached the War Memorial Building at Seventh Street. There, he slipped into a car parked along the curb. Behind the wheel was Sergei Karanov.

"Went without a hitch," Dale James boasted, slipping out of the jacket he'd worn as Mark Douglas. "Let's get outta here before it blows."

Karanov started the car and drove down Seventh Avenue. He asked James, "Did you speak to Darling?"

"Affirmative. He's on his way to see his sister right now. Said something about having brunch at her place, so they'll be together for a while."

"Excellent!" Karanov said as he waited for a light at Church Street. Although they were more than five blocks from the courthouse and the car windows were rolled up, the men heard the time bomb's powerful blast as it echoed throughout the downtown area.

"That should give a few people second thoughts about trying to fuck with El Chocomil." James sniggered as the light changed and Karanov drove on.

"So it should," the Russian agreed.

Once they reached Broadway, they headed west to Sixteenth Street, then a few blocks south to Music

Row. The rest of Karanov's makeshift army was sitting on a patio across the street from a tour bus depot. Karanov parked in a dirt lot near an idling bus. Signaling to their cohorts, he and James joined a line of tourists waiting to board the bus.

As the others crossed the street, Karanov listened to the sales pitch of a pretty young woman dressed in a cowgirl outfit, who explained that the upcoming tour would whisk people past the homes of such famous country stars as Eddy Arnold, Barbara Mandrell, Conway Twitty and Johnny Cash.

And Roxanne Darling.

12

Located off Franklin Pike in the luxurious Oak Hill area south of Nashville, Roxanne Darling's country home was a sprawling nineteen-room mansion resting on thirty-three acres of land backed by the meandering Belle Creek. A great stone gate stood at the foot of a driveway several hundred yards long, but even from the road it was possible to see the huge house resting on a knoll, surrounded by stately old oaks and younger sycamores. There were horse stables behind the mansion. White wooden fences marked off the various pastures where Roxanne's fifteen thoroughbreds roamed.

"And this is my favorite place," she told Jack Grimaldi, wrapping up the grounds tour by gesturing to a huge garden off the south wing of the house. Framed by impressive boxwoods, the garden featured huge azaleas and camellias blossoming in a rainbow of colors amid clusters of rhododendrons and peonies. In the middle of the greenery was a circular pool filled with lilypads and *koi* fish. Roxanne sat on a wooden bench overlooking the pond and motioned for Jack to sit beside her.

"Man alive, this is some place," Jack said, whistling softly as he joined Roxanne. "And I thought me and the guys had a nice spread back in Maryland."

"That was a wonderful place in its own way," Roxanne said. "I have a lot of good memories from then, Jack."

For the half hour Grimaldi and Roxanne had been together, neither of them had broached the subject of the past, sticking instead to small talk. But now that Roxanne had broken the ice, there was a sudden, uneasy lapse in the conversation. They stared into the lily pond, watching the fish cavort in the greenish water, living blurs of red and orange.

"You threw me for a loop singing 'Rescued from the Roundup' at the Opry," Jack said finally.

"Good," Roxanne said, chuckling awkwardly, "because you certainly took me by surprise, too. I almost felt like one of those people in 'This Is Your Life'."

Grimaldi said, "It's a nice song."

"The best ones come from the heart, they say." Roxanne sighed. "I always felt a little guilty about it, in a way. Like maybe I should have cut you in on royalties or something."

Jack looked at her. "Are you kidding? The flattery alone was worth it."

"It wasn't meant as flattery," Roxanne insisted. "I was just telling the truth. Jack, those few months were very important to me. You taught me a lot. A lot of things that stuck with me all these years. I'll never be able to thank you enough."

"Well, the feeling is mutual," Jack confessed. "But aren't we forgetting something here?"

"What do you mean?"

"I think you know, Roxanne."

Roxanne glanced away. The hint of tears welled in her eyes and when she spoke her voice was slightly choked. "I can't pretend that some of the things you said to me at the end didn't hurt, but I've tried to forget that part."

"And I've been kicking myself for thirteen years wishing I could have some of those words back," Grimaldi told her. "God, I can't believe what a jerk I was!"

"You had a right to feel the way you did."

Jack shook his head vigorously. "No. No way. It was jealousy, pure and simple. Italian macho bullshit all the way."

"Whatever the case, Jack, it's behind us." Roxanne put a hand on Jack's knee and he felt as if an electrical charge were going through him. "What happened to you after that? I have no idea at all."

"Guess," Jack answered lamely, not wanting to get into his misadventures with the Mafia and his present job with Stony Man Farm, at least not right away.

"Let me see," Roxanne speculated. "I know how you were always fond of planes. I bet you settled down and got yourself a job with one of the airlines. Right? I see you flying to all these exotic locations around the world and staying over between flights."

"You're close," Jack said, readying some autobiographical details that wouldn't stray any farther from the truth than necessary. "I'm a pilot, all right, but not for the airlines. I did some charter flying for a while, then got into repossession for a few years. Now I work for a private firm. Courier service."

"Do you like it?"

Jack nodded. "Every day's different. You don't get stale." Boy, was that an understatement, he thought to himself. "I got a week off and decided to stay in the States for a change. Came here on a whim and...well, here I am."

"A simple twist of Fate," Roxanne murmured, quoting from a Bob Dylan song that had been popular at the time of their courtship.

"So," Jack said, laying his hand on top of hers, "what about the present? What do we do now?"

"How about brunch?" Roxanne said, leaning over and giving Jack a light kiss on the cheek. Bounding to her feet, she waved to her brother, who appeared on the patio.

As they trod together up the flagstone path to the house, Grimaldi felt at a loss. Part of him wanted to take her hand or drape an arm across her shoulder, but he didn't want to appear too forward. Anyhow, he still wasn't sure of his feelings toward her. After so many years, he knew that he was superimposing a lot of personal fantasies from the past into the present situation, and he couldn't tell if he was misleading himself. Take it slow, he told himself. Give it time. Take baby steps.

"I hope you don't mind my inviting Brian," Roxanne said.

"No, not at all."

"He called me this morning and told me about the talk you guys had last night. Whatever it is you discussed, it sure seemed to have eased his mind. He sounded the best he has in weeks."

"That's good," Jack said. "It was just a little man to man..."

"Anyway, thanks for that, too."

"My pleasure."

Jack figured that Brian hadn't yet told his sister about his ulterior motive for going to San Leon. But from the look on the younger man's face as they joined him on the patio, Jack knew that Brian wasn't going to hold the secret back much longer.

Next to the table was a serving cart laden with a variety of breakfast rolls, bagels, fresh fruit, coffee, juice, and small pats of cheese. As Jack and Roxanne loaded their plates, Brian produced the lyric sheet he'd received at the Crusade for Conscience meeting. He told Roxanne, "I think you better fasten your seat belt, sis, 'cause I've got an earload to lay on you...."

"EVERYBODY HAVING a good time?" the cowgirl in the front of the tour bus asked the crowd, some of whose members offered affirmatives and some unenthusiastic murmurs. Many of the tourists were leaning against the windows with their cameras, anxious to get good shots of the homesteads of the rich and famous.

Karanov and Dale James sat in the front of the bus, while Fernando Carlenmach and Dennis Gent were at the back. Halfway down the aisle was a fifth member of the gang, Dale's father, Lee B. James, a wiry yet powerful man with an ill-fitting black toupee that almost matched the dyed natural hair around his ears. All five gang members were wearing slightly oversize jackets, buttoned up in front.

As the driver turned off Franklin Pike, the cowgirl resumed talking, her words amplified by a microphone pinned to her lapel so she could hold on to an upright bar for support and still have one hand free to point out the sights.

"Right now we're turning onto Sycamore Lane. It will take us through South Hills Estates, which is part of Oak Park and one of the most beautiful areas in all of Nashville. We'll be seeing four designated homes during this leg of the tour, starting just up the block with—"

Suddenly, the bus driver applied his brakes, and the vehicle came to an abrupt halt. The cowgirl, nearly losing her balance, had to cling to the bar to keep from being jerked through the front windshield. There were cries and curses from the passengers as they were tossed about in their seats.

Swearing under his breath, the potbellied driver leaned on his horn and shook a fist at a Chevy S-10 Blazer that had suddenly pulled out from the shoulder and blocked the road. It had come within a few feet of being crushed by the bus.

"Put it in neutral, chubby," Dale James advised, pressing the tip of a .44 AutoMag against the driver's right temple. The gun was nearly a foot long and the man behind the wheel could see enough of it out of the corner of his eye to know that the stranger meant business.

Karanov grabbed the cowgirl, using her as a shield. "We don't want to hurt anyone, so let's all just stay calm," he shouted to the passengers.

While the riders were trying to make sense of what was happening, the other three gang members rose and brandished lightweight Colt Cobra .38 Specials, waving them so they could be seen.

"Who are you?" a middle-aged woman in one of the first rows demanded.

"We're trick-or-treaters, lady," Lee B. James taunted. "Just thought we'd get a jump on Halloween."

Two children began to wail, as much from the shock of the sudden stop as from the appearance of the gunmen.

"What are you going to do with us?" another woman asked.

"Shut up and see!" Dennis Gent told her.

"Anybody want to play hero?" Fernando Carlenmach wondered aloud, pacing the center aisle. When he heard the click of a camera, he whirled around and aimed his pistol at a thirty-year-old man trying to slip his trusty Konica under his seat. "Give me that!"

The tourist warily complied, and Carlenmach hurled the Konica to the floor of the bus, breaking the lens clear from the body.

"Everybody put your cameras out in the aisle!" Lee B. James shouted.

Still holding the cowgirl, Karanov smiled as he watched the tourists meekly comply. The men were doing a good job of instilling fear and ensuring obedience without having to draw blood. Behind him, Gent took the place of the driver and, relying on his limited experience as a trucker, got the bus rolling again. Outside the vehicle, Chuck Scott, in the blazer, waved to Gent and Karanov, and started following the bus. Inside the wagon were additional armaments, including an Ingram submachine gun and two M-203 grenade launchers. As Karanov had hoped, use of the weapons was not yet unnecessary.

However, the plan was still a long way from being executed.

13

Jay Michael was into his fifth month as security guard at Roxanne Darling's Belle Creek Manor. He was forty-one years old and still recovering from duty-related stress and trauma that had led to his retirement from the Nashville police department on a disability pension. Michael enjoyed his new job. Although it paid far less than his police salary or even what he'd made during a brief stint working security at a local Food Mart, there was little anxiety, plenty of fresh air, and only minimal responsibilities. Besides handling all deliveries to the estate and providing entry to the grounds keepers and stable hands, Michael served as a buffer between Roxanne and the public. Occasionally, aspiring singers or songwriters showed up at the gate with some farfetched notion of having Roxanne ''discover'' them and give them their first big career break. Michael invariably gave them a business card that would deflect them toward her manager. Some fans loitered in front of the estate in hopes of seeing Roxanne come or go—Michael called it the Graceland Syndrome—and he handed out small publicity packets along with a kind warning that if the folks really cared about Roxanne Darling they wouldn't get her in trouble with her neighbors by outstaying their welcome.

And then, of course, there were the tour buses. At least two a day during the slow months and up to a dozen at the height of the tourist season. Shy by nature, Michael had enough difficulty dealing with individuals or small groups. Initially terrified by each bus load of camera-clicking tourists, he would hide behind the stone gateway while the vehicles idled in front of the estate. In time, however, thanks to psychological counseling, he worked up the nerve to show himself for a fleeting moment, then for longer periods. Finally, he could stand in full view of the cameras, waving to onlookers, and even ad-libbing a few remarks with the tour guides, whom he came to know. He was so proud of his recent extraverted behavior that he began practicing one-liners, and looked forward to the arrival of each bus so he could give his next "performance."

This morning, as he saw the familiar red-white-and-blue Nashville Lines bus approaching, Jay Michael cleared his throat and combed his gray-streaked hair. He'd learned a new joke the day before, and he was primed to try it out, grateful that he'd have the help of his favorite tourist guide, Francine.

Stepping into the middle of the driveway, Michael put on his best smile and waited for the bus to slow to a stop along the street.

It didn't.

Instead, the vehicle veered suddenly toward the gates and picked up speed. Michael stared up, horrified and confused. Where was Francine? Who was that driver?

Before the guard could snap out of his disorientation, the bus hurtled through the gate, buckling the vertical metal bars under its massive chassis. At the last possible second, Michael's reflexes took over and he tried to lunge out of the vehicle's path. The front bumper clipped him sharply and he spun away like a swatted fly, landing on the grass, hip and right leg shattered. The bus rolled another twenty-five yards up the driveway before stopping on the lawn.

Something was wrong, terribly wrong. Michael's entire body was burning with pain, but somehow he found the strength to reach for his holster and withdraw a service revolver. As he attempted to prop himself up, he heard a sound behind him and saw the Chevy Blazer pulling into the driveway. The man behind the wheel had a submachine gun.

"God help me," Michael whispered through his pain as he sat upright. Raising his revolver, he fired one shot through the Blazer's front windshield. Then the Chevy bore down on him. This time he had no way to avoid the crushing impact.

AT THE SOUND of the crash, Grimaldi interrupted Brian's confession to his sister, exclaiming, "What the hell was that?"

"I don't know," Roxanne said worriedly, looking up from the table. "It sounded close."

Although the mansion blocked the view of the front yard and driveway, Brian instinctively sensed the danger he had brought upon his sister. "Damn it, I knew this would happen!" he gasped, pushing away from the table.

"What would happen?" Roxanne said. "What's wrong?"

"If we're lucky, nothing," Grimaldi said. He led the Darlings across the patio to the corner of the house, where a boxwood shrub provided a screen through which they could see the two vehicles that had entered the estate. Farther down the driveway, Jay Michael lay facedown on the ground, his body twisted like a broken doll.

"No-o-o..." Roxanne whispered hoarsely.

Grimaldi put a finger to her lips to silence her. His eyes were on the two vehicles. A man with an Ingram was standing in the front stairwell of the bus, and on the lawn another figure cradled what looked to be a rocket launcher in his arms. A third man, standing next to the open front door of the Blazer looking toward the house, raised a bullhorn to his face, but lowered it as shouting ensued from the front steps of the mansion.

"What is the meaning of this?" came the voice of Roxanne's butler. He was answered by a single gunshot. Grimaldi had to place a hand over Roxanne's mouth to muffle her cry as they heard the sound of a body toppling down the front steps of the mansion.

An uneasy silence fell across the grounds.

"We have a very simple proposal, Ms Darling," the man with the bullhorn finally called out in a calm voice. "We know you're in there. If you and your brother come out with your car keys and your hands up, no one else will be hurt. If you don't, we start to kill the tourists.''

For emphasis, the man in the front of the bus dragged the cowgirl into view and planted the tip of the Ingram against her chest.

''Oh God,'' Brian murmured helplessly. ''Oh God...''

''He's not going to be much help right now,'' Grimaldi said as he pulled the Darlings away from the shrub.

''Who are they?'' Roxanne asked faintly, her voice trembling, her face ashen. Grimaldi suspected she was in shock over the shooting of her servant.

''That's not important right now,'' Jack said. His mind was racing, already geared into a siege mentality. ''Roxanne, do you have any guns in the house?'' he asked, feeling powerless because he was unarmed.

She shook her head.

''You have three minutes!'' came the amplified voice in front of the house. ''Don't bother trying to call the police, because your phone isn't working!''

Grimaldi looked skyward and visually tracked the telephone lines from the house to a pole situated near the main road. The lid of a service box mounted atop the pole was hanging wide open. Jack grabbed a portable phone from one of the patio tables and found no dial tone, confirming the bad news.

''I have to go,'' Roxanne said, gathering her strength. ''I can't let them kill anyone else.'' Despite her resolve, she was crying. "Poor Jay and Anthony."

"Let me go alone," Brian said. "I'm the one they're really after."

"They said they wanted us both," Roxanne said. She fumbled through her jeans pockets, pulling out a set of keys to her Dodge Lancer. "We have to do what they say."

"Wait," Grimaldi said, trying to piece together the situation. Recalling Brian's explanation that a stranger had given him the folk song by David Keliersa, Jack guessed that the incident had been a ploy to get the Darlings together. And whoever they were, the conspirators couldn't have picked a better spot to make their move than this isolated country road. Anyone driving by could be gunned down, or even ignored, since it would take far longer than three minutes to get help. The kidnappers had set up what seemed to be a foolproof hostage situation, and Jack had to conclude that they were professionals. Therefore it was unlikely that they would make any foolish mistakes. On the positive side, however, Grimaldi knew from his experience with kidnapping and hostage situations that pros were less likely to panic and start a bloodbath without provocation. But how could he, alone and unarmed, prevent the gunmen from escalating the tragedy? It was possible but not probable that they might not know what Brian looked like, but since there was little resemblance between the two men, any thought of masquerading as Roxanne's brother was out of the question.

"Two minutes!" the man in front warned.

"We can't wait any longer!" Roxanne said. Impulsively, she kissed Grimaldi on the lips. "I love you, Jack. Pray for me."

He wanted to protest against the Darlings' surrendering themselves but realized there was no other way to resolve the situation. As he watched them walk around the corner, their hands in the air, he felt a bitter tightening in his stomach. All these years of reckless courage and risk taking, often on behalf of people he barely knew, and now he stood powerless to assist the one woman he had ever loved. Goddamn it, there had to be something he could do.

But what?

AFTER DRAGGING Jay Michael's body behind the stone gateposts, Dale James and Fernando Carlenmach hauled the broken gate away so it wouldn't be seen by passersby. Should anyone make the mistake of stopping to see why a bus had been parked inside the Darling estate, the two stood guard at the entrance with their Ingrams.

Chuck Scott sat in the driver's seat of the bus with an M-203 grenade launcher, ready to blast either the bus or any law enforcement vehicle that might happen upon the scene. The latter didn't seem likely for a while because, as the hijackers figured, the bombing at the downtown courthouse had drawn most of the area's lawmen.

In the bus, there was plenty of quiet sobbing and fearful breathing among the hostages, who couldn't look anywhere without seeing a gun that would be used on them if they moved from their seats. Chuck Scott and Lee B. James were keeping a careful watch on the tourists.

Standing beside the Blazer and watching the mansion, Karanov was about to raise the bullhorn to announce that another minute had passed when Roxanne and Brian walked around the side of the house with their hands above their heads.

"Ah, very good." Karanov tossed the bullhorn into the front seat of the Blazer and drew his Beretta automatic. Raising his voice, he called out to the Darlings, "Now I want you to unlock the trunk of the sports car and open the lid."

As Roxanne went to the Dodge, which was parked just outside the garage along with Brian's Nova and Grimaldi's rental car, Karanov signaled for Lee B. James to bring him the female tour guide. James shoved the cowgirl from the bus and motioned her toward Karanov with a wave of his gun. The girl meekly complied, and the Russian grabbed her and held her in front of him before stepping clear of the Chevy.

"Now," he told Roxanne and Brian, "start the engine, then leave it running and climb into the trunk."

While his orders were being followed, Karanov moved slowly toward the car, using the cowgirl as a shield. He eyed the windows of the house, wary of anyone who might be trying to play hero. He saw no one and guessed that the death of the servant had sent an effective message to the rest of the help.

By the time he reached the Lancer, Roxanne and Brian were both in the trunk. Roxanne looked out at Karanov with pleading eyes. "If it's money you want, I can just—"

"There's nothing to say," Karanov told her. "Lie down."

Brian said, "Let her go. It's just me that you want."

"Quiet!" Karanov slammed down the hood, closing the Darlings in.

The tour guide let out an involuntary gasp of horror.

"You'll kill them!"

"Not necessarily," Karanov said. He tapped the closed hood and told the Darlings, "You might want to brace yourselves. We have a bit of a ride ahead of us."

He brusquely pushed the cowgirl aside and climbed in behind the wheel. Equipped with the Turbo Sport Package, the Dodge was packed with power. Karanov cranked the steering wheel, stepped on the gas and in a moment was clear of the driveway. Instead of heading for the road, he began circling the house. The tires chewed up the lawn, spraying loose dirt and grass as the Lancer sped toward one of the riding trails that led down to Belle Creek.

As he was passing the garden, Karanov noticed a blur of movement to his right. An instant later, Jack Grimaldi leaped onto the front hood and grabbed for a finger hold in the recessed area set aside for the wipers. He deliberately put himself directly in the line of Karanov's vision.

"Idiot!" Karanov howled, jerking the steering wheel back and forth, trying to shake the intruder free. He could hear his human cargo in the back tumble from side to side, but Grimaldi wouldn't budge.

His view disrupted, the Russian had no choice but to slow down and lean to one side to try to see where he was going. He also turned on the wipers and the windshield washer. Cleaning solution sprayed the glass but just missed Grimaldi, and the wipers refused to budge under the weight of the man clinging to them.

When Karanov tried braking the Lancer suddenly, Grimaldi held steadfast, so he reached for his gun and pointed it at the man on the hood, hoping to scare him off. Jack gambled that there was no way the Russian was going to risk losing control of the vehicle by blasting out the windshield, and he continued to hold on.

Finally Karanov saw his big chance and veered off the trail, driving dangerously close to the trunks of low-hanging boxwoods that lined the dirt path. The branches snapped loudly as they encountered the car's hood, and the sturdier limbs slapped and jabbed at Grimaldi's back, drawing blood. He tried to withstand the assault, but finally one bough clipped him soundly behind the head and he lost consciousness even as he was losing his grip. One last sharp turn and Grimaldi rolled from the hood, landing hard on the trail. Karanov drove on, leaving his foe sprawled in the dirt, unmoving.

ONCE THE DODGE disappeared behind the house, the other hijackers immediately prepared for flight. Chuck Scott slid behind the wheel of the Blazer wagon and was quickly joined by Carlenmach and the Jameses. In the bus, Dennis Gent closed the doors, turned off the engine, then crawled out a window. By the time he dropped to the ground, the Chevy had already circled around to pick him up. He piled in and Scott gunned the engine, heading back to the main road.

As expected, there was an extended period of anarchy aboard the bus as the passengers exulted in their sudden freedom and clambered to retrieve their cameras from the aisles and to be the first ones out. One woman and four men tried to assert themselves as leaders of the pack, but they were outnumbered by the hysterical majority, and valuable time was lost before the first few climbed out the same window Gent had used. Others banged open the emergency windows next to their seats and tumbled to the ground.

Francine, the cowgirl, rushed over to the body of Jay Michael and wept. She was soon joined by several others, and someone gently laid a sweater over the corpse. Two men, checking on the condition of the servant on the porch, turned him over to see blood seeping from the chest wound that had taken his life. A maid burst through the front door and screamed at the sight of her fallen colleague.

Once they had left the bus, the few self-proclaimed leaders who had gone unheeded earlier were able to round up followers to undertake separate tasks in the aftermath of the hijacking. The elderly, along with those few people who had been injured during the bus's sudden stop or the climb out the windows were encouraged to stay near the bus and wait for help to arrive. Two groups started down the road in opposite directions in search of a phone to notify the authorities.

Another group of men headed toward the back acreage of Belle Creek Manor, following the tire tracks left by the Dodge Lancer. One of them had retrieved Jay Michael's revolver, and the others grabbed whatever makeshift weapons they could find.

"I'm gonna pound that fucker within an inch of his life if'n I get ahold of him," a tall, gangly man vowed to no one in particular as he tightened his grip on a hoe taken from the side of the garage. The others fueled themselves on with similar bravado as they proceeded to the nearby horse trail.

"Damn, lookit the way he swayed along here!" someone cried out as the tracks zigzagged on and off the path, then veered off into the dogwood. "Musta been tryin' to kill those poor folks in the trunk!"

"Hey, over there!" another man shouted, pointing at the bend in the trail just up ahead.

Cautiously the men approached Jack Grimaldi just as he was waking up. His clothes were torn and he was bleeding in countless places, including his face. There wasn't one spot on his body that wasn't in pain. He tried unsuccessfully to get up on his feet.

"That him?" he heard someone mumble behind him.

"Better not take no chances," another said. "I say brain him a good one and hold him for the coppers."

With much effort, Grimaldi slowly turned around and saw three men fanning out to surround him. One of them was pointing a gun at him and didn't look as if he'd ever fired one before.

"Who are you?" the gunman demanded.

Jack muttered unintelligibly, rising slowly, painfully to his knees.

"What's that?"

As the gunman inched closer, Grimaldi lashed out, ignoring his pain and concentrating on the revolver. His aim and timing were off, but he'd caught all three men so much off guard that he was able to knock the gun loose and pick it up before they so much as took another step toward him.

"I'm on your side, damn it!" Jack said through his clenched teeth as he stood up and glared at the men. "Now let's keep going...together."

The others quickly acceded to his authority and the four of them followed the trail another quarter mile, past the fenced-in pastures and through a small wooded area before finally coming to Belle Creek, which gurgled through a streambed choked with boulders and fallen trees. The Lancer, its engine off, its doors and trunk open, was parked along the embankment in a small clearing. There was no trace of Karanov or his hostages.

"I'll be damned," one of the men muttered, scratching his head.

Grimaldi moved past the men and stumbled into the creek. The cold water rushed past him as he waded across and climbed up a gentle slope that led to a thick forest. A few yards in, he found a dirt road winding through the trees. Off on the shoulder were tracks where another vehicle had parked.

He also found blood.

Lots of it.

14

Schwarz and Blancanales had convinced Lyons they'd
be better off getting a good night's sleep before returning to Stony Man Farm, so the men were only
halfway home the following afternoon when Kurtzman reached them via cellular phone. Lyons was
driving their rental car and Blancanales was napping
in the back seat. Gadgets took the call.

"Bear? What's up?"

"You obviously don't know," Kurtzman told him.

"Know what?" Schwarz said.

"All hell's breaking loose in Nashville and Grimaldi's caught up in the thick of it."

"What?" Schwarz said.

Tipped off by the look on Gadgets's face, Lyons
said, "Click the speakers on. I want to hear this."

Schwarz activated the phone's minispeakers. By
now Pol was up in back and leaning forward to listen.
Kurtzman's voice came through with clarity and ur-
gency.

"Apparently some San Leon extremists hired out a
goon squad to try spooking some organization known
as the Crusade for Conscience. They set off a series of
small bombs in downtown Nashville while the group

was having an outdoor meeting. One dead so far, eleven injured, most of them seriously.''

"What about Jack?" Blancanales asked.

"He's in the hospital, pretty banged up," Kurtzman explained, quickly adding, "Thing is, he got put through the wringer on the other side of town trying to foil a hostage takeover at some country singer's mansion."

"Christ, you weren't kidding," Lyons said. "The two things connected?"

"Seems like it from here, but we aren't positive yet."

"What about this takeover? What was Grimaldi doing at some hotshot's...?"

"Ever heard of Roxanne Darling?"

"Of course!" Lyons exclaimed. "Who hasn't? Hell, she and Grimaldi used to have the hots for... Wait, okay, I think it's starting to add up."

"Good. In any event, the chief wants to brief you a little further and then send you in. Where are you?"

Schwarz scanned the Virginia countryside outside his window, picking out a road sign. "Coming up on Warrenton. Give us a half hour and we'll be there."

"Brognola will pick you up at the rental place," Kurtzman said.

After the Bear had hung up, Schwarz spoke for Able Team, wondering aloud, "Nashville? What the hell are terrorists doing running around in Nashville?"

JACK GRIMALDI WINCED as the nurse spread more ointment on his back, then began covering the wound with a gauze dressing.

"Yeowwww!" he groaned.

"Sorry," the woman in white told him, taping the last patch into place. "If it's any consolation, you didn't need any stitches, so you won't have scars once everything heals."

Grimaldi caught his reflection in a nearby medicine cabinet. Half his body was wrapped, including a wide band around his forehead that nearly drooped over his left eye.

"I look like Son of Mummy."

"A little," the nurse said. "But you're feeling better than when we brought you in, aren't you?"

"I feel like I went ten rounds with a blender. And lost." Jack eased back in his bed. He had an antiseptically white private room with a view of the city, including the raised spire of Landmark Center, Nashville's oldest skyscraper.

"Well, why don't you just relax? We'll bring you lunch while we're waiting for X rays."

Grimaldi groaned. "All you're going to find out is that my head's empty. I know nothing's broken."

"We'll have to let the doctor be the judge of that, won't we?"

"I guess we don't have a choice, do we?"

"I'm afraid we don't."

Once the nurse was gone, Grimaldi let down his wisecracking facade and stared blankly at the television mounted on the wall at the foot of his bed. A few minutes ago, while he'd been getting precautionary shots, painkilling injections and the mummy treatment, he'd heard a preemptive news segment about the downtown bombing and the kidnapping of the Darlings. They were being handled as part of the same story, linked by a call put through to a local news station by someone representing the San Leon Freedom Party, an obscenely inaccurate tag for what Grimaldi knew was an arm of San Leon's El Chocomil. The SLFP claimed responsibility for both incidents and threatened more bombings in other cities as well as the execution of their two hostages unless a ransom of six million dollars was paid and six of the group's so-called "political prisoners" released from United States jails where they were behind bars for terrorist activity.

The television reporter explained that no official response to the demands had yet been issued, and that neither police nor federal investigators had come forward with information suggesting that they were making any significant progress in dealing with the crisis. Grimaldi snapped off the set and crossed his arms with frustration.

What had happened to Roxanne and Brian? He shuddered at the thought of them being bounced around in the trunk of the Dodge. Even if they'd survived that, what chance did they have with their captors?

Their captor.

The face of the man in the Dodge came back clearly to him. Back at Roxanne's, the two of them had faced off for a seeming eternity, eyeball to eyeball with only a sheet of glass between them. At the time, Grimaldi had had other things on his mind than making an identification—things like survival. But now, recalling the man's face, he felt a gnawing sense of familiarity come over him. Add a little hair, take away the tan, put on a little weight in the cheeks....

"Shit!" he murmured, feeling a fresh jolt of pain as he leaned over and grabbed the phone from the nightstand next to the bed. Picking up the receiver, he made the first call that would put into motion the subsequent screenings and reroutings that would eventually put him through to Stony Man Farm. He had to let the Team know whom it was dealing with.

WHEN ABLE TEAM arrived at the Sperrytown rental agency to return the car, Brognola was waiting in Stony Man's newest transport vehicle, a customized Plymouth Grand Voyager minivan. In addition to refinements under the hood, the Voyager had been equipped with an interior computer system and detachable inner paneling that allowed for the secret storage of weapons in molded recesses.

"Just got it on Saturday," Brognola explained as the others piled in. "Thought I'd do the honors for its maiden voyage."

"Looks even nicer than it did on the drawing board," Lyons said as he checked the storage compartments and ran his fingers along the polished stock of a secreted M-14 rifle.

Schwarz started up the computer unit as Brognola pulled away from the lot and turned onto Highway 211, taking them toward Shenandoah National Park and the secret refuge of Stony Man Farm. Gadgets told Brognola, "Kurtzman gave us the headlines. Anything new in the small print?"

"Quite a bit," Brognola said. "First off, I just got off the phone with Grimaldi. You'll never guess who's running the Nashville goon squad."

"El Chocomil," Schwarz said. "We already knew that."

"True, they may be calling the shots from afar," Brognola admitted, "but are you ready for this? The local action's being handled by Sergei Karanov."

"What?" Blancanales and Schwarz exclaimed simultaneously.

"You gotta be kidding, Chief," Lyons said.

Brognola shook his head, easing the Voyager up the winding slope of the Pinnacle, a 3,700-foot peak near the Skyline Drive turnoff. "Grimaldi got a good look at him. He's the one who took the Darlings captive. From what we've been able to piece together with the FBI and CIA, it sounds like he pulled together a gang of old cronies for the job."

"Some KGB people, no doubt," Lyons speculated.

Brognola said, "The Ruskies are denying any involvement."

"Surprise, surprise," Lyons said. "Of course they wouldn't admit it. Better to slip a few favors to El Chocomil and let them grab all the headlines."

"Don't forget it's likely that Karanov's cut ties with the East," Brognola reminded the Ironman. "This might be playing to Soviet interests, but with Brian Darling linked up with this Crusade for Conscience that has been snooping around Central America, my guess is El Chocomil's acting on its own.

"In any event, things seem to be at a standstill for now. There haven't been any more bombings and the San Leonians in prison here in the States aren't going anywhere. No sightings of either Karanov, the Darlings or the goon squad. It's like they all snapped their fingers and disappeared. The President's scheduled to give a 'We don't deal with terrorists' speech in about an hour, and that might change things."

"Yeah, and probably for the worse," Lyons grumbled.

"Carl, I'm surprised at you," Brognola said. "I would have thought that you'd back a hard-line stance on this."

"In principle, I do," Lyons said. "But why bait those bastards with a lot of rhetoric? I think we'd be better off stalling for time until we can move in and hit 'em where it hurts."

"So do I," Gadgets said, still fingering the keyboard of the van's computer linkup. He was running programs in conjunction with the car's built-in phone system, and he took up the receiver to give to Brognola. "I'm patching through to the White House. See if you can't get him to back off the saber rattling at least until we have a chance to get to Nashville."

"Tall order," Brognola said, as he took the phone.

"After yesterday's fiasco, he owes us," Lyons said. "Tell him that."

Once he'd identified himself on the phone, Brognola was put through to the President and he passed along Able Team's request. The men in the van watched their chief intently, trying to gauge his reaction. When he wanted to, Brognola could freeze his features into an emotionless mask.

"Hmmm, uh huh...yes, sir...yes, yes...of course. I understand, sir. And I'm sure my boys will, too. We'll keep in touch. Good day, sir."

Brognola handed the receiver back to Schwarz and turned his attention back to driving the last stretch of Skyline Drive leading to Stony Man Farm.

"Well?" Lyons demanded. "Enough with the suspense already."

"Yeah, Chief," Gadgets badgered. "What'd he say?"

A slow grin crept across Brognola's face. "I know this is going to sound like déjà vu, but you've got twenty-four hours to get to Nashville and see what you can come up with before he moves in and does things his way."

"Twenty-four hours," Blancanales groaned. "Not again! What is this, some new game show?"

"No game," Brognola insisted. "This time, it's for real all the way."

"Good!" Lyons said decisively. "I like it when we play for keeps."

15

The Percy Priest Reservoir, just north of Smyrna, is the largest body of water in the Nashville vicinity, the centerpiece of a fourteen-thousand-acre recreation area created by the Army Corps of Engineers. With a meandering shoreline that provides thousands of separate inlets, the facility assures privacy to all who seek it. Even the private property next to the park is remote, particularly the farther one ventures from the primary roads.

Years ago, Lee B. James had paid cash from a bank heist to purchase a small plot of land in what he considered to be the most isolated niche of the Percy Lake region. Separated from the reservoir by a rugged, almost impenetrable forest, and from any neighboring homes by swampland, the two-room shack James built served periodically as a hideout when he wanted to escape from the rat race to hunt or fish. Even after he and his son had migrated eastward in search of better opportunities around Knoxville and Oak Ridge, James had held on to his property, not only because it was difficult to sell, but also because it proved useful as a place to store hot property and, on several occasions, bodies until they could be buried.

And now the small cabin was being used by Sergei Karanov.

Having abandoned Roxanne Darling's Dodge at the edge of Belle Creek, Karanov had transferred his bruised and bloodied captives across the stream to a Nissan Maxima he had rented earlier under an assumed name. Then, with the prisoners secured in the Nissan's trunk, he had driven without incident to the hideout. As a precaution, the car was parked in a shed behind the cabin.

Because the James property was continuously shaded by surrounding pines, the house was cool even before dusk crept across the marshes. Karanov fed kindling and small blocks of hard pine into a Franklin stove in the corner of the main room and watched as flames began to eat at the wood. The shades were drawn, and the fire helped a small table lamp fight off shadows that filled the shack with a sense of gloom.

"Ah, that's better," he told himself, going into the cramped kitchen, filling a kettle with water and setting it on the stove. Then, wiping a layer of dust from a sturdy wooden rocker, he sat down. Beside him was a cardboard box filled with provisions, from which he took and opened a bag of salted cashews. Munching them one at a time, he watched his prisoners.

Both Roxanne and Brian were bound to chairs across the room, and both had bruises and swollen faces from their ordeal in the trunks of the Lancer and Maxima. They were neither gagged nor blindfolded. A scab was forming where Brian had split his lip, and a bandage covered the gash on Roxanne's forehead that had bled so much back at Belle Creek. They sullenly watched Karanov eat.

"You'll like this place better once it warms up," the Russian said jovially.

"I hope that's what they tell you when you go to hell," Brian snapped angrily.

Karanov laughed. "Nice to see you can keep a sense of humor through all this." He maintained a trace of his Texan drawl even though he was sure the prisoners weren't taken in by the deception.

"What do you want us for?" Roxanne asked.

"For information and leverage mostly, I'd say. And a ransom, of course." Karanov let his gaze slowly wander along the gentle curves of Roxanne's figure. "Who knows? Maybe for a little pleasure, too."

"Don't you dare!" Brian threatened.

Karanov smiled and threw a cashew across the room, striking Brian in the ribs. "Oh, but I might."

"You won't get away with this," Roxanne said. "You have to know that."

The Soviet shook his head. "My dear, I'm not in the habit of doing things I can't get away with." He turned to Brian. "How about if we have a more profitable conversation, hmmm? Perhaps about this Crusade of Conscience you belong to, Brian, and all your nosing around in the affairs of San Leon."

"Forget it," Brian said.

"That's no attitude." Karanov finished the cashews and started in on a ripe pear, noting the looks of hunger his captives were trying to hide. He took another piece of fruit from the box and held it out in front of him. "Hungry?" he asked.

Roxanne shook her head. "If you're holding us for ransom, how are you supposed to keep in touch with anyone out here in the middle of nowhere?"

"But how do you know we're in the middle of nowhere?" Karanov teased. "You were blindfolded when you got here and the windows are closed off. I might have just taken you for a long ride and brought you back to a place down the street from your mansion."

"You're not answering my question," Roxanne said.

"Well, if you must know," Karanov said with a sigh, removing a portable shortwave radio and microphone from the provisions box, "I plan to use this. But first I need to have something to tell my people."

Brian shouted, "Tell them they can all go—"

With unexpected swiftness, Karanov leaped from his rocker and reached his prisoners in one long stride. He struck Brian with so much force that he toppled over, chair and all, landing on the hardwood floor. Leaning over, Karanov grabbed the younger man by the ear and nearly tore it from his head as he seethed, "Enough patty cake, Brian. I want to know your contacts in San Leon. Besides David Keliersa, who is very, very dead just now."

"Leave him alone!" Roxanne pleaded. "Please!"

Karanov ignored her and banged Brian's face against the floor, reopening the wound on his lip and forcing his nose to bleed as well. "Do you understand me? I want information!"

"No!" Brian cried out through his pain. "I won't talk!"

Karanov roughed Brian up further, cuffing him with his fists, then kicking him in the ribs. When Roxanne screamed, the Russian turned on her, lashing out with the back of his hand and raising welts across her cheek with a sharp blow that nearly bowled her over as well. Taking the rag he'd used to clean the rocker, he gagged her, snickering at the choking noises she made.

"Fine, fine," Karanov said, breathing heavily from exertion. "I can see that you need a little added persuasion. That can be arranged."

Karanov strode out the front door, giving the Darlings a glimpse of Tennessee twilight before the door closed. They heard him opening the car.

Brian had finished telling Roxanne about El Chocomil while they were being driven to the hideout, and although he felt an overwhelming guilt at having pulled her into the turbulence of his personal affairs, he had been grateful for her understanding. As he looked up at her from the ground, blood streaming down his face, he weakly told her, "This is what they do every day to hundreds, thousands of people. This and worse! They have to be stopped."

Roxanne nodded, tears wetting her bruised face. She looked at her brother with anguish at his bloodied condition. Then, out of the corner of her eye, she noticed the shortwave radio and pointed it out with nods of her head until Brian turned.

Six feet away.

Lying on his side bound to a chair, Brian had limited flexibility, but he found that by wriggling his body he could inch forward without the chair legs making too much noise dragging across the floor.

Five feet.

Four...

The rope bit and sawed into his flesh with each movement, increasing his agony beyond anything he had ever endured.

Three feet.

Two.

He blinked away the blood that was clouding his vision. Once he reached the radio, he would still have to figure out how to get his hands on it, and how to use the mike and broadcast a message. Spurred on by hope and desperation, he began contorting himself, rising to his knees and reaching the last few inches to the radio dials.

From outside came the sound of the Nissan's hood slamming and Karanov heading back. Brian reached the dials and began fiddling with them blindly. He hadn't even found the power switch when the door opened and Karanov stepped inside.

"Very resourceful, Brian, but also very futile."

Karanov was carrying the car's battery as well as a set of jumper cables. He set them down next to Roxanne, then nonchalantly took the radio from Brian's reach and uprighted him in his chair.

"I don't suppose you changed your mind while I was gone," Karanov said as he went to the kitchenette for a large bowl.

"Fuck you!" Brian cried out in his frustration.

"I didn't think so. No matter, because I think I have a way to loosen your tongue."

Karanov pulled off Roxanne's shoes and socks and put her bare feet in the bowl. Whistling, he took the kettle from the stove and made sure that Brian could see the steam rising from its spout. As he poured the scalding water into the bowl, Roxanne let out a passionate scream that was only partially muffled by her gag.

Then Karanov hitched up the jumper cables to the battery and held the opposite ends apart. Looking at Brian, he brought the ends together, creating a spark of electricity. When Karanov pried open the cable clamps and slowly drew them close to Roxanne's arms, the younger man cried out, "Don't! I'll talk! Damn it, you bastard, I'll talk!"

16

As it turned out, there was a positive payoff to Able Team's false arrest in Washington. When a Stony Man pilot dropped them off at a remote hangar at Nashville Metropolitan Airport shortly after sundown, the three men were greeted on the tarmac by Jesse Rolow, the FBI's top man in Tennessee. Affable by nature, the thin, handsome agent went out of his way to endear himself to the Team, welcoming each member warmly, showing none of the territorial wariness they usually encountered whenever they wandered onto another agency's turf.

At first, the trio took the glad-handing in stride, but once inside Rolow's Olds Cutlass, Lyons couldn't help but wonder. "I take it your boys in D.C. told you to put on the kid gloves, eh, Rolow?"

The agent grinned as he paid the parking attendant and pulled out onto Murfreesboro Pike, heading for town. "Yeah, you could say that," he admitted. "They musta pulled some kinda royal boner with you guys, right?"

"Right."

"Not gonna tell me?" Rolow asked. "Listen, 'tween you and me, our Washington boys sometimes get a little carried away with themselves, y'know? Like there's still a little too much Hoover in the air out there.''

"Well, hallelujah," Lyons muttered. "Somebody else notices D.C. folks are a little off."

"So, what'd they do?" Rolow persisted.

Lyons briefly explained the circumstances of the false arrest, and Rolow howled with pleasure at the comeuppance his fellow officers had received. Then Blancanales changed the subject, asking Rolow if the Bureau had made any headway on the case.

"Matter of fact, yes." At the next overpass, Rolow linked up with Highway 40, which took them, appropriately enough, past three cemeteries. He told the others, "We ran a check on those stiffs that got iced down in Memphis. At the Banner Hotel?"

"Yeah, we heard about them," Lyons said.

"One of them was a guy named Jimmy Lou Bowline," Rolow explained, "and the other guy has so many aliases we aren't sure what his real name is, although we do know he's KGB. Supposedly he's the one who did the exterminating."

"This time it looks like the exterminator got to him first," Gadgets speculated from the back seat. "Karanov, no doubt."

"That's what we figured after we checked our files, too. Karanov and Bowline crossed paths a few times over the years."

Lyons thought things through and said, "If Karanov bumped off the guy sent to nail him, you can bet he's looking to skim off a nice slice of that ransom money so he can pull a Houdini before the next betrayal."

"By the same token," Blancanales said, "if we can just get our hands on one of those flunkies that helped hijack the bus, we could spoil ol' Sergei's vacation plans but good."

"We're working on that, too," Rolow said. "We got descriptions from the passengers and did some cross-referencing on Karanov's file. Made a positive ID on a Dennis Gent. He's another KGB contract man, very low level. We also placed him in Memphis during that business at the Banner. Had a room there under a bogus name. We think that's where this whole Nashville thing got cooked up."

Rolow exited off the downtown business loop and drove to Memorial Hospital, telling Able Team, "Death count from that bombing's up to two now, and there's another gal that could go any minute."

"Has Karanov given any details about how he expects to have the money delivered?" Schwarz asked as they left the car and headed for the main entrance of the hospital.

"He wants it all in small unmarked bills," Rolow said, "and he wants it on the same plane with the terrorists he wants released. He won't say where he wants 'em delivered until there's confirmation that we'll meet the terms."

Blancanales glanced at Schwarz and Lyons. "I wonder if we could pull the same sting we did with the dons?" He was referring to one of their recent cases in which they had masqueraded as syndicate bosses released from prison as a condition to keep the Mob from unleashing nerve gas into the air over Yellowstone National Park. By the time the ruse had been discovered, Able Team had gotten close enough to the Mob hideaway to eliminate the threat.

"Only as a last resort," Lyons said. "Karanov's covering all the angles too closely to let us pull a fast one on him. We'll have to find another way."

Entering the hospital lobby, the four men spotted Jack Grimaldi sitting in a wheelchair by the check-in window. His clothes covered most of his bandages, but not his gauze headband which surrounded his scratched and bruised face.

"Goddamn, am I glad you're here!" Grimaldi told them. "Hurry up and wheel me out so I can get out of this friggin' chair!"

"You can't pilot a wheelchair on your own?" Lyons teased. "Not a good sign, Jack, buddy."

"You want a good sign, Lyons?" Grimaldi snarled, flipping him the finger. "How's this?"

"I believe the man's on the road to recovery," Lyons proclaimed.

WITH THE FIRE BLAZING in the Franklin, the cabin was warm now. Roxanne had collapsed from fatigue and was asleep in her chair, oblivious to the ordeal her brother was still enduring.

"What else?" Sergei Karanov asked Brian as he calmly jotted notes on a small pad.

Brian, weakened from the interrogation and from his wounds, was leaning heavily against his ropes.

Hunger tore at his stomach, tying it in knots. "That's all I know," he whispered through his parched lips. "I . . . I need water, a drink. You promised."

Karanov reached for the plastic bottle of spring-water nearby and, tilting the bottle back, swallowed the last of its contents, smacking his lips with exaggerated pleasure. Looking at Brian, he threw the bottle, striking his prisoner in the face.

"There!" Karanov chuckled. "Refreshing, isn't it?"

Brian's eye began to swell where the bottle had hit it. He swallowed hard, feeling dried blood crack along his neck. When he tightened his lips, the cut bled some more and the fluid moistened his tongue, bringing forth a little saliva. He wasn't going to ask Karanov again. Not for water or for food. Better to sleep, let his exhaustion overtake him, and allow him to regain some strength. He felt so tired, so spent, so ashamed for having divulged his secrets about the Crusade's connections in San Leon. He knew that his cooperation had saved his sister's life, but for how long? Had he only forestalled the inevitable?

"Sleepy," he murmured to himself, bowing his head forward until his chin was resting on his chest.

Karanov watched him nod off and was about to revive him when a voice came over the shortwave. It was Lee B. James, using truckers' jargon in a prearranged code to keep Karanov abreast of what was happening beyond the confines of the cabin. Karanov responded in kind, using his Texas accent and speaking with the carefree ease of a semi driver rolling home after the biggest haul of the year. To an eavesdropper, their conversation must have sounded like that of two good buddies shooting the breeze as they knocked off miles on their eighteen wheelers. However, between the lines, James was notifying Karanov that there had not yet been any official response to the demands, although the President had been quoted as saying that the safety of the hostages was the primary concern. It wasn't what Karanov had expected. He'd been counting on the President refusing outright to deal with the kidnappers. He told James to contact the media with word that the Darlings were still alive but that their captors' patience was reaching an end. Then he signed off. Staring at the flickering fire, Karanov considered the situation.

His instincts all along had told him that the United States would never meet with terrorist demands of the magnitude that Karanov had proposed. He hadn't expressed these misgivings to Juan Guandaro because of their shaky friendship, and also because Guandaro, through Miguel, had saved him from the KGB in Rio. Karanov knew that, all else being equal, Brian and Roxanne Darling were more valuable to him alive than dead. If the United States refused to pay ransom or release prisoners, as Karanov believed would be the case, then he could turn around and cut a deal with Guandaro that would be worth even more than the generous terms that were already on the table.

Surely, Karanov would tell Guandaro, you would rather have the pleasure of avenging your brother's death personally. I can bring him to you alive . . . for a price. His sister, too.

If the United States appeared to comply with his demands, that would foul everything up because, in fact, Karanov had no hard plan for following through on a ransom exchange. He was familiar enough with kidnapping cases to know that kidnappers are eventually apprehended, usually when they tried to collect the ransom. Of course, he could demand that the prisoners and money be flown to San Leon and parachuted into the hills before he released Roxanne and Brian, but then he would have to contend with Guandaro for his share without any leverage.

No, it was better for him to kiss off United States, keep the Darlings and work out something with Guandaro. That would be more of a business transaction between friends than a kidnapping. Fewer complications.

Karanov used the shortwave to contact Lee B. James. Still using the truckers' parlance, he informed his cohort that he'd changed his mind and wanted the media to know that because the government was stalling, the stakes had been raised. Now, in addition to the earlier demands, El Chocomil wanted the United Nations to pull out of San Leon immediately so that the country could "benefit from the purity of self-determination." There was no way the President could consent to such terms, and even if he did, Karanov knew that the U.N. wouldn't follow suit. If Guandaro were to accuse him later of asking for more than the agreed-upon terms, Karanov figured he could merely claim that the American government had fabricated the final U.N. ultimatum as an excuse to back away from meeting any of the demands.

Karanov signed off with James and looked over at his sleeping prisoners, stifling a yawn. He figured that he should get some rest, too. Tomorrow he would abandon the cabin and drive off to another location, known to himself.

There, safe from any possible betrayal by James or the others, he could wait out the collapse of the ransom talks, then make arrangements to sneak back to Central America with his Darling little pawns.

But before he could sleep, there was a small matter he wanted to attend to. As Miguel had prevented him from having his way with the show girl back in Rio, Karanov's peculiar appetite for carnal gratification had not recently been satisfied. The events of the past week had demanded most of his attention, but now he could indulge himself. Of course, killing Roxanne first was out of the question, but there were ways of simulating the rush that came from his signature form of lovemaking.

Taking a full bottle of springwater, Karanov walked over to Brian and spilled it over the man's head. Brian sputtered back to consciousness, coughing and spluttering. At first dazed and disoriented, he soon recalled where he was.

"There's your drink, Brian," Karanov taunted, unbuttoning his shirt as he stepped over to where Roxanne was asleep on the floor. "Goodness, it sure has gotten warm in here, hasn't it?"

When Brian saw the Russian crouch beside Roxanne and began to unfasten his belt, he cried out, "No! Stay away from her! I told you all you wanted to know!"

"Don't worry," Karanov told Brian assuringly as he stroked Roxanne's ruffled hair, then her cheek. "I'm not going to kill her...."

"Please, leave her alone!" Brian begged.

Karanov continued to fondle Roxanne until she began to stir. Then he glanced back over his shoulder and told Brian, "Watch. You might learn something...."

17

Given the plethora of intelligence and law enforcement agencies operating throughout the country, it is not surprising that sometimes it seems the left hand does not know what the right hand is doing on even the highest-priority cases. Thus, when Jesse Rolow took Able Team and Jack Grimaldi to the FBI's Nashville field office, the Bureau team was at its wits' end trying to coordinate all the additional "help" being channeled into the local crisis.

When Rolow asked fellow agent Marty Bass if things were as chaotic as they looked, the second man threw up his arms with frustration. "On top of all the official agencies throwing in their two cents' worth," he complained, "since we publicized mug shots and offered rewards on the two Jameses and this Gent fella, we're getting ten calls an hour from people claiming they've seen 'em. So far, they're in Memphis, St. Louis, Smyrna, Franklin, Shelbyville and just about every town between the Appalachians and the Mississippi. We try following through on all these 'leads' and we aren't going to have anyone left to answer the goddamn phones!

"And if that isn't enough, we just got word the ante's been upped on the Darlings. Now those fucking Freedom Party clowns want us to pull our U.N. forces outta San Leon. Jesus, you'd think they were goddamn ball players going through free agency!"

Bass's outburst was heard throughout the room, turning heads and drawing attention to the new arrivals. Grimaldi and Able Team took in the wary glances of the other FBI agents, feeling about as welcome as a strain of Legionnaires' disease.

"Well," Lyons told Bass with unveiled sarcasm, "now that you've passed out the party favors, I guess we should start having ourselves some fun, right?"

Bass lit a cigarette and blew smoke from his mouth and nose. As the other officers returned to their work, he eyed Able Team and mumbled, "Look, I had to blow off some steam. Nothing personal, okay?"

"No blood, no foul," Blancanales said.

Schwarz pointed to a back room, where an untended bank of computers was visible through gray-tinted windows. He told Bass, "If you got a log of those calls you've been getting, I can start punching them into a computer."

"Think that'll help?"

"You'd be surprised," Schwarz replied. "And I can set it up so we reroute all incoming calls about suspected sightings to our people back East. With any luck some pattern will emerge and we can narrow down the search."

"What the hell, it's worth a try," Bass conceded.

"That's the spirit," Lyons droned. "Give it the old college try."

As Rolow took Schwarz to get the phone log and the key to the computer room, Grimaldi asked Bass, "Any luck on the getaway cars?"

"The Blazer was stolen two hours before the kidnapping," Bass reported. "Fifteen minutes after the kidnapping, county sheriff's people found it abandoned along a country road four miles away. Must have been other cars parked there waiting for a switch. We're canvassing the neighborhood to see if anyone saw anything, but so far no luck."

"What about the car across the creek?"

Bass shrugged. "Best we could do was get a plaster of the tracks. Standard Continentals, no distinguishing marks. Probably a few hundred thousand of those floating around this part of the state. Lightweight car most likely. Compact maybe."

"How about making a chart of all stolen cars in the area?" Lyons suggested. "Start with a half-mile radius and work your way out."

"Already on it," Bass said through another cloud of smoke. "So far there's just the Blazer and an old Buick Electra. We're checking the rental agencies, too."

Blancanales smiled, playing politician with the harried Bureau agent. "Guess we should stop telling you how to do your job, eh?"

"Not necessarily," Bass said. "You want to chip in, the red carpet's out."

"But you're not that thrilled about it," Blancanales surmised.

"Like I was saying, everybody's playing hero today." Bass sighed. "But at least you guys know what you're doing. Look, I gotta get back to it. Why don't you plug in anywhere, and let somebody know what you need?"

"We aren't here to play prima donna," Blancanales said. "Just give us some grunt work until we find our best lead."

Bass's expression changed, giving way to the hint of a smile. "You got it."

While Bass took Lyons and Blancanales into a huge workroom filled with cluttered desks, ringing phones and overworked agents, Grimaldi limped stiffly into the computer room, where Schwarz had already put several microchips under his command.

"You were pretty well raked over the coals, Jack," Gadget said, noticing that Grimaldi grimaced when he sat down.

"I feel worse than I look," Grimaldi confessed. "All I keep thinking about is that bastard forcing Roxanne and Brian into the trunk. Damn it, if I could have just somehow got him to stop that car..."

"If he had stopped, he would have rolled down his window and picked you off with that popgun you said he was toting," Schwarz reminded his colleague. "I know you, Jack. You did all you could."

"But it wasn't enough."

"Any luck, you'll get another chance." Gadgets punched out a command, linking the computer with

Stony Man Farm via a modem that would also handle transfer calls. That task completed, he asked Grimaldi, "You and Roxanne still have a spark?"

"Yeah," Grimaldi said, recalling her kiss and her last words to him. "Yeah, there was something there, all right."

"I was wondering how many times you were going to come here before you got the nerve to look her up."

"Was it that obvious?"

Schwarz nodded, and Grimaldi forced a smile despite his anxiety. Glancing over Schwarz's shoulder at the monitor he asked, "What are you doing?"

"Inputting all the sightings," Schwarz explained. "Then I'll run checks from the files on known hangouts for operatives in this part of the state. Hopefully we'll get some overlaps."

The wizard hacker took his hands off the keyboard to flip through a manila FBI file, as new readings continued to flash on the screen.

Grimaldi said, "You got this sucker on automatic?"

Schwarz shook his head. "That's Bear programming the calls we diverted to the Farm."

"Man, I just can't keep up with this technology," Grimaldi said. "Unless you slap wings on it, of course."

"Of course."

"'Gent, Food Mart, Shelbyville, 9:45'" Grimaldi read off the screen, "'Lee B. James, Cowpoke Saloon, Lavergne—'"

"What'd you say?" Schwarz said, looking up from the files.

"Right there." Grimaldi pointed at the monitor. "Second row down. Middle column."

"All right!" Schwarz set aside the file and attacked the computer with a frenzy, his fingers tap-dancing across the keyboards like a vaudeville hoofer.

"What?"

"The Cowpoke Saloon used to be a drop point for Soviet agents infiltrating the Air National Guard in Smyrna," Gadgets said as he worked. "Now, unless I miss my guess, most of the sightings of James will also be around Smyrna and Lavergne."

"I don't believe it," Grimaldi said.

"Why not?"

"I know that area," Grimaldi said. "Hell, the Cowpoke's a hard-nose country bar where you can't get in unless you're decked out looking like you just walked off a Marlboro ad. You can't tell me the KGB's got people working out of there."

"It's in the file," Schwarz told him. "The drops were usually in a field out back, near where the Stones River feeds into the Percy Priest Reservoir...and look at the screen here. Three sightings of somebody who looks like old man James in just the past few hours."

"I say we go for it," Grimaldi said, anxious to take the offensive.

"We? You're a walking Band-Aid, Jack," Schwarz reminded Grimaldi. "You can't go running around like that."

"Watch me," Grimaldi said.

"Well, if that's the way you want to play it." Schwarz left the computer and rose from his chair. "Let's check with these people and see if they have some extra Western threads lying around. We've got some cowpoking to do."

18

Although several reported sightings of Dennis Gent had come from many places near and including Tennessee, the man was actually holed up in a dusty hotel near Billings, Montana. Fernando Carlenmach had crossed the Texas border and was reveling in a Mexican whorehouse. Chuck Scott was on a fishing trawler in the Gulf of Mexico, swilling Coors on the poop deck as he waited for marlin to bite his bait. Of those who had participated with Sergei Karanov in the treachery in Nashville, only Lee B. and Dale James, father and son claiming to be descendants of the notorious James brothers of Missouri, had remained behind to see the drama through. For their dedication, Karanov vowed to pay them forty-five thousand dollars more than what they'd already earned. At first it seemed like a tidy sum, but later Lee B. wasn't so sure.

"All these millions they're talking about and we're riskin' our asses for diddly-squat!" he complained. "Hardly seems right."

He and Dale were in a room at the Lavergne Dewdrop Inn, just off Industrial Boulevard. The younger man, fully dressed, was lying on one of the twin beds, fanning himself with a stack of fifty-dollar bills. "It's like you used to tell me all the time growin' up, Pa. Bird in the hand's worth two in the bush. Man, check out this cash! I ain't seen this much in one place since we rolled that faggot in Atlantic City."

"Yeah, but it's just a spit in the bucket compared to what Karanov's gonna walk away with," Lee B. said. He was eyeing himself in the bathroom mirror and dabbing tanning lotion on his face. He'd already abandoned his toupee and trimmed what little there was of his natural hair, leaving his scalp showing through an inductee crew cut. "I think I oughta tell him we want bigger shares . . . or else."

"Forget it, Pa," Dale told him. "Shit, he's the one put us back on our feet when you got outta the pen last time and couldn't scrounge up any decent scratch no matter what you tried, remember?"

Lee B. whirled around and pointed a warning finger at his son. "Don't be puttin' me down, Junior. I told you about that a hundred times if I told you once. *I'm* your old man, not him!"

Dale rolled his eyes and tucked his bankroll back in his pocket. "What's that got to do with anything?"

"I get sick and tired of you sidin' with him against me all the time. 'Karanov this,' 'Karanov that.' Commie bastard kissed some Ruskie ass and got himself a little clout. So what? Don't make him better than me!"

"Who said it did?" Dale sat up, his legs dangling over the edge of the bed. "All I'm saying is he's the one callin' the shots on this one and we already made a deal. Why fuck things up gettin' greedy?''

"He's the greedy one!" Lee B. insisted. "And the fucker's stayin' tucked away at *my* place while I'm out here playin' errand boy and stinkin' up my face with this tan shit so I don't look like that mug shot of me in the goddamn newspaper!''

"Tan, my ass," Dale chortled, standing up and stabbing his feet into a pair of lizard-skin cowboy boots. "That crap's turning your skin orange, Pa. You look like you got a pumpkin where your head's supposed to be.''

"Mouthin' off again?" Lee B. slammed the quick-tan tube into the wastebasket and glared at his son. "You little bastard, I shoulda stuck you with your Ma like she wanted. You deserve each other, fuckin' ingrates!''

Dale slipped on a coat and headed for the door. "I don't need this grief, okay?''

"Where you think you're goin'?"

"Out!" Dale told his father, pulling a small index card from his pocket. "I'm supposed to call the cops in twenty minutes, remember? Ain't about to do it here.''

"You just better watch your ass," Lee B. said. "They're out lookin' for you.''

"Yeah, yeah.''

"Long as you're out, get some more smokes. And stop by the Cowpoke for a couple meatball subs.''

"You just had one a couple hours ago," Dale said.

"So maybe I got a tapeworm. Just do it, wouldya? You can pretend you're gettin' 'em for Uncle Karanov."

"Enough with the guilt trip, Pa, okay? I'll get 'em."

Dale left, cursing his father under his breath as he walked to the parking lot. What was the old man's problem, anyway, aside from the fact that he was a loser and didn't want to own up to it? Just jealous of Karanov, that was all. Maybe he was worried his son would learn a thing or two from the Russian and end up making something of himself. Wouldn't that be a real kicker, for him to wind up a big shot and maybe hire out his own father for a job some point down the line? Give the fart a taste of his own medicine.

Dale grinned at the prospect, then promptly pursed his lips so he could whistle with admiration at the sight of a sharp-looking black Trans Am parked near the hotel office. He'd wanted one since he'd seen Burt Reynolds speeding around in a double bill of "Smokey and the Bandit" movies at a Knoxville drive-in.

He briefly considered hot-wiring the car and taking off in it, but there were people in the office and, besides, he and his old man planned on staying here at least another night. Instead he hopped on the Suzuki 1000 he'd driven to Nashville earlier in the week.

The Dewdrop was located near an old industrial park crowded with warehouses and small factories, and there was continuous truck traffic around the loading docks. Opening up the throttle, Dale raced past several rigs and a new housing development going up half a mile from the hotel. Turning onto a dark country road, he inched up the speedometer, enjoying the rush of cool wind past his face. He sang "Born to Be Wild" at the top of his lungs. He was thinking about what to do with the money in his pocket as well as the windfall still to come. Maybe he'd buy a Trans Am and drive it to California, hit Hollywood and ball a few budding starlets, then get discovered by some talent guy and end up on a TV series. Man, the people there made some real money, every fucking week. Yeah, that could be a real nice gig. . . .

He slowed down as he approached an intersection where the shops and gas stations on all corners had closed for the night. A few hundred yards past the crossroads, a great deal of noise was spilling out of the Cowpoke Saloon.

Pulling into a gas station next to a phone booth, he left the bike running as he fed a few coins into the phone and dialed a local number.

"Police, southwest station."

"This is Chocolate Milk," Dale muttered the code name for the kidnappers through a handkerchief held over the mouthpiece. He was reading the message from an index card Karanov had given him. "Don't talk. Listen. The deadline's been moved up. We want an answer by morning. Meet all terms or the Darlings are dead meat."

"Wait, we want to—"

James slammed down the receiver knowing that a short call was nearly impossible to trace. Returning to his bike and goosing the throttle, he yanked up his front end and did a wheelie onto the road. Then he eased the tire back down and skidded to a stop in the parking lot of the Cowpoke Saloon.

"WELL?" LYONS ASKED Grimaldi. "What do you think?"

Grimaldi looked over his Able Team cohorts, who had changed into Western duds appropriated from the Bureau's undercover division. "You guys look like the Three Amigos."

"Close enough," Blancanales said. "Let's hit it."

The men, not wanting to bog themselves down with an unwieldy backup force, had downplayed the significance of the Cowpoke Saloon to Rolow and Bass. Without mentioning specifics, they told the Bureau agents they merely wanted to check out a few sightings in the Smyrna/Lavergne area. Remembering their orders from Washington, Rolow and Bass gave the Team access to their car fleet. Able Team opted for a nondescript Pontiac Bonneville and a Honda Accord hatchback, breaking into two groups to avoid drawing suspicion by traveling together. Grimaldi and Schwarz led the way in the Honda while Lyons and Blancanales followed at a safe distance in the Pontiac. In slightly more than twenty minutes, they were in Lavergne, pulling up to the Cowpoke Saloon.

The parking lot afforded a clear view of the front entrance, where a bouncer the size of a sumo wrestler checked IDs and frisked all incoming patrons.

"Shit!" Lyons said, removing a Government Model Colt from his waistband and sliding it under the front seat of the Bonneville. "So much for going in armed."

He and Blancanales took one final look at the mug shots of Sergei Karanov, Dale and Lee B. James and Dennis Gent, then left the car and walked past a Suzuki 1000 to the front door, where Grimaldi and Schwarz were already being patted down by the bouncer. Jack winced each time one of his wounds was slapped.

"What happened to you?" the bouncer asked him gruffly.

"I was gored by a runaway bull," Grimaldi claimed.

"Yeah, right."

"I may look bad," Grimaldi joked, "but you oughta see the bull. Turned that fucker into a La-Z-Boy recliner."

The giant chortled with a deep laugh that almost drowned out the stage band's half-baked version of "The South's Gonna Rise Again." "You're in luck. We got rid of our bull a couple years ago."

"You ate it, right?" Schwarz said, eyeing the bouncer's considerable girth. The big man didn't look pleased with the wisecrack, so Gadgets took it back. "Just kidding, just kidding."

After paying a cover charge, Grimaldi and Schwarz entered the bar. The place was vibrating from the high-decibel output of the band, which played on a raised stage in the corner, separated from the dense crowd by a barrier of chicken wire.

"Man, does this bring back memories," Grimaldi said, noting a few crumpled beer cans, wadded napkins and stray french fries stuck in the wire mesh.

"What?" Schwarz yelled above the din.

Grimaldi shook his head. "Never mind. Let's spread out."

The four men spread out, milling slowly through the crowd in search of the suspected kidnappers. With all the Stetsons, brawl scars, sideburns and mustaches in the place, it quickly became evident that if the fugitives were disguised, they would be almost impossible to find.

A buxom waitress with a no-nonsense look and more makeup than Tammy Bakker, nearly collided with Grimaldi while carrying a tray filled with drinks.

"Clear the runway, Mac," she told him impatiently. "You wanna drink, I'll get ya on the way back."

As Grimaldi let the woman pass, his gaze fell on a stocky man behind the bar, emerging from the kitchen with a grease-spotted take-out bag, shouting, "Meatball subs to go!"

Dale James, leaning against the counter, waved to get the cook's attention as he finished his beer. Grimaldi recognized him instantly.

As James took the bag and headed for the exit, Grimaldi glanced around in search of the men from Able Team. Spotting Blancanales, he motioned to James and then followed him through the crowd toward the exit. Packed as the bar was with drunken dancers, it was no easy chore, and Grimaldi took so many elbows to his wounded body that he felt like a bruised pear after a produce sale.

By the time Jack reached the parking lot, James was already straddling the Suzuki, with the take-out order tucked inside his jacket. Grimaldi had a quick decision to make. Should he detain James and wait for the others? Or should he get in the car and follow him, hopefully to Karanov and the Darlings?

As James revved the Suzuki, Grimaldi strode quickly to the Honda and got in. He fired the ignition and put the Accord into gear. James thundered out of the lot and rolled down the road. Grimaldi followed. In his rearview mirror he saw Able Team rushing out of the bar to the Pontiac.

19

Dale James had a rearview mirror, too. When he saw one, then two sets of headlights following him, he pushed the Suzuki to its limit. The bike sped down the dark country road, distancing him from the other vehicles. In less than a quarter mile, James was doing eighty-five, ninety, ninety-five miles per hour. When he glanced at the mirror fixed to his left handlebar and saw the headlights actually creeping closer, he knew for sure that he was being followed.

"Son of a bitch!" he howled at the wind, trying to plot his next move as the speedometer crept toward three figures. Up ahead, a lighted billboard advertised the turnoff to New Horizon Village, the housing development under construction down the road from the Dewdrop Inn. He eased up on the throttle, slowing down the Suzuki as he inhaled deeply in preparation for the risk he was about to take.

As soon as he sighted the side road, James snapped off his lights. He was beyond the reach of the headlights behind him, and if he could handle the upcoming turn without applying his brakes, there was a chance he could lose his pursuers.

"Come on, baby," he coaxed the bike as he shifted his weight in the seat. Still barreling along at more than forty miles an hour, James swerved sharply to his left, leaving the main road. There were concrete pillars flanking the entrance to New Horizon Village, and the biker came within inches of splattering himself against the imposing uprights. Rather than raise a dust cloud on the unpaved road, he remained on the grass shoulder, heading toward the half-built homes in the distance. He shut off the Suzuki's engine so that he couldn't be heard from the main road. He figured that once he rolled to a stop, he could leave the bike behind and head to the inn on foot.

Chancing a glance over his shoulder, James swore at the sight of a car making the same turn he'd just taken. When he looked forward again, he was appalled at the sight of a sewer line scooped out of the earth immediately in front of him. He tried pulling up the front end of the bike, but with the engine off he couldn't get any additional thrust. Instead of clearing the gully, the front tire dipped and slammed into the opposite embankment. Carried along by its momentum, the bike somersaulted end over end, throwing James over the handlebars. He hit the ground headfirst, snapping his neck. The Suzuki landed on top of him, and would easily have killed him if he hadn't already been dead.

The Honda slowed and stopped in the dirt, and its brights shone on the wrecked motorcycle. Jack Grimaldi jumped out of the car and ran to the fallen biker. It didn't take him long to realize he wouldn't need the gun that was in his hand.

"It's Dale James," he told Able Team as they piled out of the Pontiac.

"Damn! So much for him leading us anywhere." Lyons looked around at the half-built homes at the end of the road. "I wonder if the others are holing out in one of these model homes?"

"I doubt it," Schwarz said as he helped Grimaldi search the dead man, finding the thick wad of fifties that had filled Dale James with dreams of grandeur.

Jack found the take-out bag nearby. "Two hot sandwiches," he said. "Seems a safe bet he was heading somewhere close. Someone's probably waiting for him."

Looking past the housing complex, Blancanales noticed a few semis on Industrial Boulevard. "Looks like a lot of factories that way. We could be looking for a needle in a haystack."

"I don't think he was hiding out in a factory," Grimaldi said, removing a hotel key from James's coat. "There's a room number on this key, but no name. We'll have to check a phone book."

Schwarz emptied James's jeans pockets and held something up to the headlight beams. "Then again, maybe we won't," he said.

He was holding a matchbook advertising the Dewdrop Inn.

LEE B. JAMES STUFFED his loose clothes into a well-worn leather satchel, then glanced at his watch. He didn't have much time before Dale would return.

Dale, that inconsiderate, uppity excuse for a son. Always sucking up to the fucking Ruskie. *Karanov showed me this. Karanov taught me that. That's not how Karanov would do it.* Well, fuck Karanov. Lee B. James didn't need to play no goddamn second fiddle to anyone, 'specially a Commie. Not anymore.

He had a plan.

The papers had publicized that the police were offering a reward for information leading to the arrest and conviction of the Nashville terrorists. A hundred grand. James figured he could call the Feds, tell 'em he knew where Karanov was hiding. Possibly he could pretend he had been working undercover for the CIA or something, trying to see how many KGB agents he could round up for arrest. That might get him off the hook. If they didn't buy it, he could at least get some immunity from prosecution in exchange for talking. Yeah, do a little horse-trading—testimony in exchange for some dollars and a new identity in the witness relocation program. With a new name and a bit of status, maybe he could even find a nice broad and get hitched again. He could disown Dale after the bastard went behind bars with dear Uncle Karanov.

"You're onto something, Lee baby," he told himself in the mirror. "Gonna hit the big time."

His bag packed, James was about to leave the room when the door burst open and four men charged in, overwhelming him before he could even open his mouth. He found himself pinned to the bed by two of the intruders. A third man turned on the television real loud, while the fourth, with short blond hair and penetrating blue eyes, loomed over him, screwing a silencer onto the barrel of a Colt .45 automatic.

"Okay, partner," Carl Lyons said as he wrapped a pillow around the pistol. "First we'll blow off your kneecaps, then your elbows. If that doesn't inspire you, we'll go for the ankles and wrists. You've got five seconds to think about it. Five . . . four—"

"Wait! Wait!" James said. Even through the pillow, he could feel the hard, round tip of the silencer pressing against his knee. "Gimme a fucking chance, willya? I don't even know what the fuck you're talking about!"

"Three . . . two—"

"Jesus, all right!" the orange-faced man bartered. "I was planning to talk anyway. Go easy, why don't you?"

Lyons demanded, "Are the Darlings still alive?"

James bobbed his head. "Yeah, last I heard."

"Where?"

"Close by," James said. "Get off me and I'll let you know. Hell, I'll take you there if you give me a bleedin' chance!"

AFTER THE ABUSE Sergei Karanov had inflicted upon her, Roxanne Darling pretended she was sleeping, but in reality she was wide awake, filled with anger, shame and revulsion. These were new and unfamiliar emotions to her, and she was frightened by their ugliness. Part of her wished Karanov to be executed in such a slow and painful way that he would experience some of the degradation she felt. At the same time, so brutal a hunger for vengeance alarmed her. How could things have come to this? Only a day ago she was on top of the world, feeling as well as she ever had. Full of hope and happiness for the future. Now that future seemed impossibly bleak.

When he had forced himself upon her, Karanov hadn't even bothered to untie her, and she still lay on the floor, strapped to the chair, her clothes torn and disheveled. In contrast to the warmth emitted by the Franklin stove, the floorboards were unbearably cold, bringing chills to her half-naked body. But she kept her eyes closed and willed herself to ignore her discomfort and pain. She had to devote her full concentration to survival, to holding on to what little hope there was.

Finally, to her right, she heard the sound she had been waiting for. Karanov's breathing had become rhythmic, with a catch to it, a sort of half snore rustling through his nostrils.

Was he really sleeping? she wondered. Or was he pretending as she was, tempting either of his captives to act so he could again torment them with the futility of their situation.

She shifted slightly, as if changing positions in her sleep. Now she could see the Russian, sitting in the rocker across from her, head tilted, gun in his lap. His eyes were closed and his lower lip hung outward, opening his mouth just enough to amplify his snores.

Turning the other way, she saw Brian, still bound to his upright chair, weeping quietly. When he noticed that Roxanne was awake, he began to sob.

Unable to whisper to him through her gag, Roxanne could only shake her head and tell him with her gaze to be quiet. Somehow he understood her gesture and fell silent, although his eyes still betrayed the depths of his misery.

During his frenzy of lust, Karanov had inadvertently knocked over the Nissan's battery and neglected to right it. Acid slowly trickled from the individual cells onto the floor, eating into the wood. Only a few feet away, Roxanne found that she could creep and maneuver toward it even though tied to the chair.

When she reached it, she inhaled deeply and began to pray as she rubbed her rope-bound wrists along the top of the battery. Acid burned her flesh. The pain was as excruciating as any injury she had yet suffered at the Soviet's hand. But it was easier to take, knowing that the liquid also ate into the rope. Roxanne felt she would pass out from the chemical burns ravaging her palms and wrists. But suddenly she felt her bonds give way, and her joy outweighed the agony.

First she yanked the gag from her mouth, then fumbled with the knots securing her ankles to the legs of the chair. Covering herself with her tattered clothes, she crept to her brother and unbound his wrists. He was able to help with the knots around his legs and ankles, and soon he, too, was free.

They embraced for an instant, then she whispered in his ear, "Let's go."

"Not yet," Brian whispered determinedly.

"Please."

"There's something I have to do first."

Looking for a weapon, Brian picked up the jumper cables, disconnecting them from the overturned battery. Then he wrapped the ends tightly around his hands, creating a makeshift garrote. Crossing the floor, he closed in on the man in the chair.

The moment the cold cable pressed against his neck, Karanov jerked awake. The motion sent his gun tumbling from his lap to the floor. Brian put all his strength into choking the Russian, but even his rage was not sufficient to snuff the Soviet. Karanov pushed Brian's hands away from his throat and kicked him in the stomach, propelling him backward. Brian reeled over a fallen chair and sprawled to the floor.

"Oh, you'll pay for that!" Karanov shouted.

He was rising from the chair when Roxanne heaved the half-empty battery at him. The projectile bounced off his jaw, but most of the impact was absorbed by his collarbone, which cracked under the sheer weight and momentum. Knocked off balance, he fell to the floor and was temporarily immobilized by a rush of pain radiating from his shoulder.

"Come on!" Roxanne shouted to her brother, jerking him to his feet and leading him to the door.

Outside, in the darkness, they ran in a blind panic. They reached the shed where the Nissan was parked, but with no key and no battery it was of no use to them. So they continued on, brushing painfully against several trees before finally stumbling upon a path.

"FOOLS!" KARANOV HOWLED as he emerged from the cabin, carrying his gun. His prisoners were gone. "There's no way you'll be able to hide from me!" he shouted into the night. "You had a chance to live longer, but now you will die!"

Familiar with the lay of the land, Karanov was confident he would catch Roxanne and Brian the moment they betrayed their position. He waited near the back steps, listening to the sounds of the woods, finally hearing his prey thrashing through the trees to his left, behind the shed. Releasing the safety on his gun, the Russian ran to the shed, where he retrieved something from the Nissan. Tucking the object into his back pocket, he started walking silently along the dirt path leading into the forest.

Despite his rage and his wounded shoulder, Karanov found reason to smile. This was a situation that embodied the very essence of his livelihood—the stalking of the game. And it wasn't like the recent assignments that had made him so weary of the KGB. This time his target wasn't some inanimate secret document or formula but rather flesh and blood. It reminded him of his proud days as a prized assassin. This was his element. His instincts came alive and he breathed deeply, bringing his pain under control.

The hunt was on.

20

It took Jack Grimaldi only five minutes to drive from the Dewdrop Inn to Smyrna Air Center. He reached the bar there, Bill's Landing, only a few minutes before closing, and luckily found Milt Nieton caught up in a game of darts with several other Air National Guard officers.

"Jack!" Nieton exclaimed. "What the hell are you doing back here at this godforsaken hour?"

"Got an emergency, Milt."

Grimaldi drew Nieton away from the other officers, quickly introduced him to Able Team and explained the situation.

"Well, shit!" the base commandant said. "If there's any way I can help, just name it."

"Good," Grimaldi said. "I knew I could count on you. For starters, we want to take a chopper up. Also, do you have any sort of night scopes?"

"No problem with the chopper," Nieton replied, "and I've got a few Startrons slapped onto Colt Commandos."

"Madre de Dios!" Blancanales muttered, genuinely impressed.

Lyons shook his head with disbelief. "Yes, Virginia, there is a Santa Claus."

"What'd I tell you guys?" Grimaldi boasted, slapping Nieton on the back. "The man's an ace up our sleeve."

"How about if we save the oohs and aahs for later?" Schwarz suggested. "We still have a lot of work to do."

AS THEIR EYES BECAME accustomed to the darkness, Roxanne and Brian quickened their pace through the dense forest. Night sounds abounded around them, playing on their nerves. The sudden wing-beating flutter of birds disturbed from their nests led to the scampering of squirrels from limb to limb in the surrounding pines, and in each instance the Darlings would tense with fear and draw closer to each other.

"When does this forest end?" Brian muttered with frustration, trying to find a glimpse of light through the wooded blackness that might lead to safety from the man they knew was in close pursuit.

"Come on, we have to keep moving," Roxanne insisted, tugging her brother's arm.

At the edge of a sharp downward slope, the path abruptly ended. Before Brian and Roxanne was a small clearing, in the middle of which was a deserted campsite. A crude circle of small rocks surrounded a fire pit filled with ash and charred bits of wood.

"What do we do now?" Roxanne wondered.

"We'll try to throw him off the track," Brian said as he crouched over the fire pit and began gathering the rocks. "You head off that way," he told his sister, gesturing into the foliage. "I'll catch up with you."

"But—"

"Just do it!" Brian insisted.

As Roxanne ventured warily through the thick growth, snapping twigs underfoot and creaking the lower branches of tall pines, Brian went the other way and began hurtling rocks in all directions. As he had hoped, the stones stirred up the wildlife as they clattered through the forest. Rabbits bolted across carpets of dry, fallen pine needles, crows cawed and beat their wings overhead, chipmunks dashed in spiraling motions up the sides of the trees, their small claws clicking against the bark like castanets.

Rushing through the brush, Roxanne moaned each time her burned hands were slapped or stabbed by the foliage. The ground dipped unevenly as she raced down the incline, and halfway down her left foot caught on an exposed tree root and she fell forward, tearing the ligaments in her ankle. Clenching her jaw, she held back an involuntary grunt of pain. Her agony was so intense that a galaxy of stars exploded inside her head and she fainted, landing hard in a thick, musty carpet of undergrowth and fallen leaves.

Brian had thrown all the stones, and as the veil of silence returned to the forest he was just starting down the slope. Thirty yards from his sister he heard her fall.

"Roxanne?"

No answer. Striding down the hill, he repeated her name. Because there was no trail, he couldn't tell which way she'd gone, and panicking, he zigzagged back and forth, hoping to stumble across her. Again he whispered her name, and again was answered by silence. Then came the sound of someone at the top of the rise.

Brian froze, afraid to move.

THE PRIDE OF THE Tennessee Air National Guard's aerial fleet was its MH-6 helicopter, a modified version of the old Hughes OH-6 Cayuse. A lightweight two-man observation chopper that in recent years had become a tactical mainstay for various United States special forces units, the MH-6 was unrivaled in its combination of quiet stealth and ability to be flown full speed at low levels in the dead of night. Jack Grimaldi couldn't have asked for a better aircraft for the mission that lay ahead.

While Able Team, following the directions of a handcuffed Lee B. James, was driving to the remote cabin behind the Percy Priest Reservoir, Grimaldi was flying across the wide, clear water, with Milt Nieton riding beside him. Nieton was readying the Startron Mark 424 night-vision system attached to the bore of his 5.56 mm Colt Commando assault rifle. The Startron was a Smith & Wesson sight, utilizing a 25 mm intensifier format that allowed for a 14.5-degree field of view. A microchannel plate amplifier further enhanced the system's effectiveness by limiting amplification of bright areas, thereby providing a more even illumination of the view.

"Chopper sure purrs like a kitten, eh?" Nieton commented as he made the final adjustments to one sight, then picked up the second.

"I'll say," Grimaldi replied, banking the copter slightly as they came within view of the eastern shoreline. "Still, I don't know how close we want to get. Karanov hears anything suspicious and he's going to be tipped off that we're onto him."

Nieton set aside the second assault rifle and used a small penlight to study a topographical map of the reservoir area, upon which Lee B. James had marked the location of his cabin. Nieton, pinpointing a possible landing point, looked out the rounded windshield of the chopper to locate the corresponding areas down below. "Looks like our best bet'll be that spit of land down there on your left, just off the cove," he said. "It's about five hundred yards from the cabin. That should be far enough."

The chopper swooped low across the smooth surface of the reservoir. Ahead, the jagged tops of tall pines rising from the shoreline were silhouetted in the moonlight, blending into the darkness of the forest. The spit Nieton had referred to was a small, thin peninsula that jutted tentatively into the reservoir, rising barely a foot above the waterline. The wind had often blown the water over the land, and through the years the surface had become not only smooth but also soft and green from moss and algae.

Grimaldi set down the flying machine on the flat area, then killed the engines. The rotors had raised ripples in the water, which made a tranquil, soothing sound that contrasted sharply with the image of the two men stepping from the copter carrying weapons capable of disrupting the serenity with 750 rpm bursts of 5.56 mm destruction.

Nieton led the way along a narrow dirt path from the spit up the imposing incline of the shoreline, with Grimaldi following close behind. Jack was not a religious man, but during the ascent he hoped that if there was a God, He would see to it that their siege would not be in vain.

"RIGHT HERE," Lee B. James said, indicating a hidden turnoff on the winding road that cut through the marshland east of the reservoir. His face was hardened and his eyes were cold, and not because of the handcuffs pinning his wrists behind his back. Although he'd quarreled with his son, the parental bond ran deep. James had a strongly personal reason for wanting revenge against Sergei Karanov. To the father's way of thinking, his son was dead because of that Russian bastard. It would give him solace during his years in prison to know that Karanov had received his just deserts.

Lyons pulled the Pontiac off the road and killed the engine. James was sitting beside him, while Schwarz and Blancanales were in back. Pol had one of the

Startron-equipped Commandos, and Gadgets his trusty Model D automatic.

"What's the best approach?" Lyons asked James.

"Another hundred yards down the road there's a break in the fence," James explained. "Go through that and you'll see a trail that threads between the marshes. It'll take you up right behind the cabin."

"Good," Lyons said. "Let's do it."

Able Team left the Pontiac and Blancanales hauled Lee B. James behind the vehicle, where Lyons opened the trunk.

"Man, you can't put me in there," James protested. "I'll suffocate!"

"If you've led us astray you might," Lyons said. "Otherwise we should be back in plenty of time. Now get in."

Prodded by a jab in the ribs from Blancanales's Commando's flash-suppressor, James reluctantly climbed in.

"You're lucky we're not driving around with you in the trunk," Lyons told him. "Think what it must have been like for the Darlings to be bounced around cross-country."

The Ironman quietly lowered the lid until the lock caught, then led Schwarz and Blancanales down the road. Thanks to Milt Nieton, they had changed from their Western outfits into night camouflage gear and Kevlar bullet-proof vests. Blending in with the rampant overgrowth along the road's shoulder, the men moved with pantherish stealth until they came upon the small opening in the fence James had mentioned.

Pulling on a loose section of fence, Lyons widened the gap so his cohorts could squeeze through without snagging their clothes. It was slow going, for the mud sucked at the men's feet, pulling them down. They waded through more than twenty yards of quagmire before reaching solid ground and, pulling themselves up, were startled by a group of mallards that burst up through the reeds and cattails.

"Damn!" Pol whispered, drawing his finger away from the trigger of his Commando. "We nearly had ourselves a year's supply of duck soup."

On the solid earth the men made better time, advancing through the brush until they spotted a curl of dark smoke rising above the horizon, betraying the location of the cabin. Shifting course slightly, Able Team reached the clearing in which the house and shed were located a few minutes later. The men were only a few feet from the shed, and once they broke clear of the reeds and high grass they used it for cover.

Through a dirt-caked window, they saw the parked Nissan, confirming that Lee B. James hadn't misled them.

"I'll case out the cabin," Pol said, inching to the edge of the shed and readying his night Startron. He aimed at the cabin and peered through the sight. It didn't take him long to assess the situation.

"Back door's wide open," he said. "Looks pretty quiet inside."

"Might be a trap," Lyons said.

"Only one way to find out."

Choosing approach angles, the three men fanned out. Holding the Commando, Schwarz went for the doorway, while Lyons and Blancanales took windows at opposite ends of the cabin. They froze at each opening, then cautiously peered inside and saw the overturned chairs and the toppled battery.

"Damn!" Schwarz muttered as he stepped through the doorway, lowering his rifle. "They're gone...."

21

The path leading from the reservoir was seldom used, and was overgrown or eroded in places, forcing Nieton and Grimaldi to trail-blaze up the steep-pitched rise. The ground was highly unstable, and at one point a shoulder of gravel gave way under Nieton. When the commander lost his footing, Grimaldi pulled his friend back onto the path. As Jack steadied himself on an outcropping of rock, his assault rifle slipped from his grasp. End over end, it bounded down the cliff and splashed loudly into the cold deep water.

"Shit!" Jack muttered.

Nieton righted himself and extended a hand. "Better the gun than us, Jack."

"Yeah, right," Grimaldi grumbled. He reached for his shoulder holster, pulling out his .45 automatic. "Good thing I brought along some backup."

The two men bypassed several other obstacles without further complications and were soon atop the rise and staring into the dense forest.

"Which way?" Grimaldi wondered aloud.

Nieton glanced over his shoulder, locating the helicopter some fifty yards below. Bearings established, he led the way along the faintest hint of a trail, taking it thirty yards into the black maw of the forest before he stopped and held up a hand to silence Grimaldi.

"Hear something?" Grimaldi asked.

Nieton nodded, slowly raising his assault rifle. Squinting through the Startron, he adjusted the focus with his left hand. Silently, he motioned for Grimaldi to check through the sights. It took Jack a moment to adjust his eyes to the distorted image in the lense, but once he was able to get a clear fix, he let out a sigh of relief.

"It's Brian Darling," he whispered. "Cover me, Milt."

Nieton took the commando back and assumed a firing position as Grimaldi headed down the path.

Brian was only twenty yards away, and when he twitched with fear at Grimaldi's approach, Jack hissed, "Brian, it's me!"

"Jack?" Terror was evident in the younger man's voice. "Jack?"

"Right here," Grimaldi said, approaching Brian.

"Oh God, thank God!"

"Shh," Jack quieted him. "What are you doing here?"

Brian quickly explained the circumstances of their imprisonment and escape, concluding, "And I just couldn't find where she fell, Jack. I looked everywhere but—"

"It's okay, Brian, it's okay," Jack said. "I've got a friend back the way I came. Go wait with him."

"What about you?" Brian asked.

Grimaldi released the safety on his Model D. "I'm going after her. And him . . ."

KARANOV HADN'T BEEN fooled by Brian's diversion with the rocks. Taking cover behind a thick sycamore to avoid being hit by a random toss, he was mildly impressed by the young man's ingenuity. And the girl's, too, for that matter. Whatever they had done to escape their bonds back at the cabin required more strength and fortitude than he would have thought possible for them. Now that it had come down to a hunt, that was good. It was always so much more rewarding to go up against worthy prey.

Once the shower of rocks had ceased, Karanov had advanced to the fire pit, where he waited for the wildlife to settle down and for his captives to once again reveal their positions. His patience was rewarded, as he soon detected movement down the west slope, heading toward the reservoir. It was only one person, he guessed. Where was the other?

Slowly he started down the incline, senses alert. He could still hear someone fleeing in the distance, but for now that didn't concern him. He knew that there hadn't been time for them to lay an elaborate trap. If indeed one of them were lingering behind, he or she was most likely behind some tree, armed with nothing more than a rock or stray branch. Sticks and stones. If he was stupid enough, there was a chance he could be attacked from behind.

"But I'm not that stupid, my pets," he muttered under his breath. "I have some tricks of my own."

Reaching into his back pocket, Karanov removed a safety flare, the object he had taken from the Nissan. It was a sophisticated torch, with a spike protruding from one end and a self-igniting tab on the other. The Russian held the stick away from him and jerked off the tab. Almost instantly, a spark-spitting ball of fire erupted like the head of a giant match, burning brightly through the dark forest.

Karanov wasn't about to carry the flare with him. Instead, he took aim at a sycamore some twenty feet away and, with the fluid grace of a master knife thrower, hurled the flaming stick so that it cartwheeled through the air and embedded itself, spike first, in the crotch of the tree.

"Now, then," he murmured, crouching low so that he was at the same level as the foliage. The flickering light filled the woods with spastic shadows, and Karanov looked hard to discern the enemy.

Instead of Brian or Roxanne, his sweeping gaze detected the luminous eyes of a nearby deer that had been momentarily spooked by the burst of light. It was a doe, large ears perked upward in alarm. As she was about to flee, Karanov swung his Beretta into firing position. He had the firing system switched to single shot, and he drilled a silent 9 mm round into the deer's neck. Death was almost instantaneous, although the creature struggled to defy the inevitable, scrambling a few yards into the brush before her legs finally gave way.

Despite a jab of pain in his shoulder from the Beretta's recoil, Karanov smiled, pleased with his aim. He moved forward, staying within the wavering glow cast by the safety flare. He rose to a higher crouch, less concerned with exposing himself than with being able to spot either Roxanne or Brian huddling in the brush.

"You can't hide forever," he called out softly.

A pronounced groan drew Karanov's attention to his left. Another four steps brought him into an area of half-light, where he found Roxanne, still crumpled in the leaves, just regaining consciousness.

"Ahh, what do we have here?" he murmured, standing over the woman. "Another doe?"

Dazed, Roxanne blinked, aware primarily of the pain in her ankle. Karanov leaned toward her.

"Get away from her, Karanov!"

Startled, the Russian glanced up. The voice had come from his left. Turning slowly, he saw Jack Grimaldi standing less than fifty yards away, pointing a .45 automatic at him. Once he overcame his initial surprise, Karanov grinned.

"You again. This woman should be grateful to have such a diligent guardian angel."

"Get away from her," Grimaldi repeated, slowly moving forward and to one side, half shielding himself behind a tree.

"But she is my ticket to freedom," Karanov explained, taking care to let Grimaldi see that his Beretta was aimed at Roxanne's face.

"I wouldn't have thought the great Sergei Karanov would stoop to hiding behind a woman," Grimaldi taunted.

"Oh, but I'm not hiding," Karanov said. "I'm in clear view. Go ahead, take your best shot. There's always a chance my gun will misfire before I drop. She could live."

Grimaldi knew better. Even if he were to get off a perfect shot and nail Karanov between the eyes, the Russian's trigger finger was more than likely to carry out Roxanne's execution even after he was technically dead. Jack couldn't risk it.

"Well, then," Karanov mused as he began to pull the dazed woman to her feet, "if you're so concerned about her life, I would suggest that you turn around and go back to wherever you came from—"

"No!" Roxanne suddenly screamed, lashing out at her captor. She managed not only to deflect the Beretta's barrel from her face, but also to shove the Russian away from her.

In the next instant, not one but a handful of bullets plowed into Sergei Karanov. In addition to Grimaldi's blast, which slammed into the Russian's face, an equally lethal rain of 5.56 mm fire chopped through his torso at a downward angle. Karanov's gun did go off as he fell to the forest floor, but the shot went nowhere near Roxanne, who also fell when her ravaged ankle refused to support her.

Grimaldi bolted past the sputtering flare and knelt beside Roxanne. She leaned greedily into his embrace, holding him tight, repeating his name over and over.

"It's okay," he told her. "It's okay."

They continued to cling to each other as Gadgets Schwarz led Able Team down the incline from the old campsite. He lowered his Colt Commando and stood over the man who had tasted the weapon's venom. To their right, the flare had nearly burned down to the spike, and its pulsating glow began to weaken. Soon darkness would reclaim the forest.

"Nice shooting, Schwarz," Lyons told his cohort. "You, too, Jack."

"Yeah," Grimaldi said, breaking his embrace with Roxanne. "Let's get out of here."

EPILOGUE

"...and thanks to Lee B. James singing his pretty little head off, we've rounded up everybody in the gang but Fernando Carlenmach," FBI agent Jesse Rolow told Able Team at the Bureau's Nashville field office the following morning.

"And thanks to you guys, too, of course," agent Bass conceded in the background. He forced a grin and added, "Not that we ain't pissed about you weaseling around behind our backs to get it done."

"Nature of the beast," Lyons chuckled. "What can I say?"

"You guys need a ride back to the airport?" Rolow asked.

"Thanks, but we've already got it covered," Schwarz said as he and his partners headed out the door.

Outside the office, Brian was waiting behind the wheel of his '73 Nova, and Roxanne's Lancer was idling nearby. Lyons and Blancanales got into the Dodge while Gadgets joined Brian. Both cars pulled out into traffic and, passing Music Row, headed down Demonbreun Street. South of the tourist traps were numerous buildings where the true gears of the Nashville music scene turned. KDI Recording Studios was a complex of five small buildings clustered together at the corner of Music Square West and Williams Avenue. The two cars came to rest in the parking lot adjacent to the main building. While the others waited, Brian got out of the Nova and went inside.

"Hello, Brian," the security guard told Darling. "Some ordeal you and your sister went through, huh?"

"I'll say." Brian took the visitor's pass the guard handed him and clipped it to his shirt pocket. "Where is she?"

"I just saw her in the lounge."

"Thanks."

Brian headed down the hallway, passing framed gold and platinum records, some of them belonging to his sister. About to enter the lounge, he froze in the doorway, seeing Roxanne and Jack Grimaldi embracing near the vending machines. Brian tactfully returned to the hallway and busied himself with inspecting the trophies on the walls.

Grimaldi, who had seen Brian out of the corner of his eye, kissed Roxanne a final time before easing from her arms. She shifted her weight back to her crutches.

"Airport shuttle's here," he said.

"Oh, shoot."

Emergency treatment and an overnight stay at the hospital had done much to alleviate her pain, although her face was bruised and both her hands and one ankle taped. She seemed in good spirits. If anything, her biggest ache came from the heart.

"You're sure you can't stay?" she asked Jack. "I'll be done with the first tracks on the album by Wednesday, then we could spend some time together."

Grimaldi sighed. "Maybe another time, okay?"

Roxanne reached out and stroked his face. "I care so much about you, Jack. I'd love to have you back in my life."

"I think that can be arranged," Jack told her. "But it'll have to be just as friends."

"But why?"

"I think you know why, Roxanne," Grimaldi said. "We live in different worlds. It'd be too much of a sacrifice for either one of us to try to find some kind of common ground on a permanent basis."

Behind the couple, the door to one of the soundstages opened and a technician poked out his head, telling Roxanne, "Ready when you are, Ms Darling."

"Okay, I'll be right there, Jerry," Roxanne said. When she turned back to Grimaldi, there were tears in her eyes. "Well, then I guess this is goodbye."

"For now," Jack said. "It won't be thirteen years between visits next time."

"Promise?"

Jack leaned forward and kissed her. "Promise."

They gazed at each other, treasuring the moment. Then Jack turned and headed away. Behind him, he heard Roxanne sniff, then start for the soundstage, softly singing.

True hearts stay close
Even when they're far away.
True hearts stay close
Forever and a day...

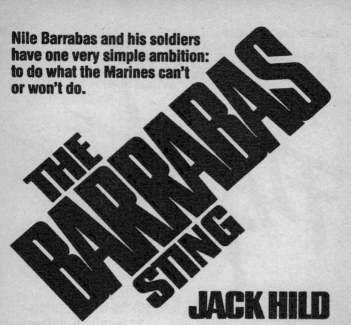

Mack Bolan's

PHOENIX FORCE

by Gar Wilson

The battle-hardened, five-man commando unit known as
Phoenix Force continues its onslaught against the hard
realities of global terrorism in an endless crusade for
freedom, justice and the rights of the individual. Schooled
in guerrilla warfare, equipped with the latest in lethal
weapons, Phoenix Force's adventures have made them a
legend in their own time. Phoenix Force is the free world's
foreign legion!

**"Gar Wilson is excellent! Raw action attacks
the reader on every page."**

—Don Pendleton

You don't know what
NONSTOP
HIGH-VOLTAGE
ACTION
is until
you've read your
4 FREE
GOLD EAGLE
NOVELS

TAKE 'EM NOW

FOLDING SUNGLASSES
FROM GOLD EAGLE

Mean up your act with these tough, street-smart shades. Practical, too, because they fold 3 times into a handy, zip-up polyurethane pouch that fits neatly into your pocket. Rugged metal frame. Scratch-resistant acrylic lenses. Best of all, they can be yours for only $6.99.

MAIL YOUR ORDER TODAY.

Send your name, address, and zip code, along with a check or money order for just $6.99 + .75¢ for postage and handling (for a total of $7.74) payable to Gold Eagle Reader Service. (New York and Iowa residents please add applicable sales tax.)

Remove from pouch...

unfold once...

GOLD EAGLE

Gold Eagle Reader Service
901 Fuhrmann Blvd.
P.O. Box 1396
Buffalo, N.Y. 14240-1396

unfold twice...

and they're ready to wear.

GES-1A

Offer not available in Canada.